"I chose this for you," Josetta had said, pulling the iron from the fire. Her voice had dropped to a whisper. "It will be how I know you." But Elanor hadn't understood, not until she felt the heat. Not until she felt the press of the iron against her back, heard her own skin blacken. And as she smelled her flesh burn, she heard Josetta's voice.

"May you be protected from the wickedness inside you. May you be guarded from your own power."

For my parents,
of whom I am equal parts made

N

E

S

Eremurus
(Home of the
Eastern
Monarch)

1 week / Carriage
1 Month / foot
3 Days / horseback

Josetta's Castle

Tunnel

1 day's walk from the Mountain

Elanor's Room
Barracks
Celebration Room
Mineral Pools
Infirmary
Altar
Dining Hall
The Mountain
trance
Kitchen
Barrier
Midlands Forest

Burn

$\mathscr{R}$ecall the four sisters

(Extraordinary! Extraordinary!)

Who fought for others to be saved

They were ravaged by a shameful war

Though their loving hearts were brave

And so a vengeful bramble

Grew thick upon their graves

Each thistle then sharpened

By the hands of former slaves

—*"The Ballad of the Four Sisters"*

Chapter .1

Elanor's shoulder was bleeding. The wound pulsed like a second heartbeat, blazing hot beneath her jacket before turning heavy and cold, blood soaking the bandage again. Rhys had removed the arrowhead days ago, but his hands had been shaking. For someone so proficient with a sword, he wasn't very fond of the sight of blood.

They should stop. Elanor looked over in Rhys's direction. They hadn't spoken since sundown, moving at a punishing pace through the forest, and in the moonlight she could see him slumping under the weight of his pack, his chin dipping toward his chest.

He was exhausted. They both were, but these woods

weren't safe for those who needed a place to rest. There were wolves and bears and other beasts, but mostly there were huntsmen. Josetta's huntsmen. And nothing ceased their searching.

Elanor knew they wouldn't be safe until they were past the barrier. Until they were home. The Queen had sought out their hidden camp for years, filling the woods with spies and soldiers. And if not for the magical barricade constructed by the Elders, and for the Orphans' constant, watchful eye, Josetta would have found them many times over. Only the Mountain was safe, and Elanor had learned long ago not to trust the world beyond it.

They were close. Elanor could smell it. The faint scent of fire and iron. Home. Her face tingled in the chilled air. Snow was on its way. That, too, she could smell, fresh and clear and sharp.

To keep herself awake, Elanor assessed her injuries. There was her shoulder, of course, but there was a host of other pains that would need to be healed. Her legs ached, and she couldn't remember when she had last removed her shoes. Every inch of her exposed skin was cold and stiff. Her face, her ears, her fingers. Winter had come on quickly during their journey; neither of them had been prepared. Elanor had a hood, but it lay limply against her neck. Pulling it up over her head might warm her, but it would also limit her sight and hearing. With exhaustion already threatening her senses, she couldn't risk another distraction. There had been too many of those already.

Elanor swallowed the bitter taste that came with the memory of the ambush. She should have been paying attention. She should have heard the huntsmen coming. Instead she had let herself be distracted by the princess and her magic. By the trees rustling and the welcoming sunlight and the bright slash of rainbows dancing across Aislynn's and Thackery's faces.

And when Elanor had finally come to her senses, it had been too late. Even now, Cinnamon's howl echoed in her ears—the low, mournful call of trouble. Why hadn't her bow been drawn? Why hadn't she reached for one of her many knives? Why had she just stood there until an arrow cut through the air and through her shoulder?

She had stumbled, might even have fallen if it hadn't been for Rhys.

"Ellie!" he had said.

How she hated that nickname.

The pain was nothing. She'd had much worse, but it was the shame of getting caught that stung. Of being surprised by a group of huntsmen so large that a hibernating bear would have heard them coming.

It was later, when she was wiping their attackers' blood from her weapons, that Elanor realized how truly unnerving the attack had been. The others seemed mainly concerned about who the huntsmen were looking for, but Elanor knew that wasn't what really mattered.

"I've never seen Josetta's huntsmen this far north before," she had said, knowing she had to turn back. The Elders needed to know what had happened.

That had been several days ago. Rhys had decided to return with her and hadn't questioned the pace Elanor set for them. They were close.

Suddenly Elanor's skin tingled with the sensation of magic. It was a bittersweet feeling, one she missed the moment it was gone. Like forgetting thirst until drinking a single drop of sweet water and then thinking of nothing but your parched tongue. That was how magic always felt to her. She heard Rhys let out a sigh of relief. They had reached the barrier.

Wide-awake now, Elanor sped up. Rhys matched her stride and they moved through the trees together, the surroundings familiar even in the dark. The branches above them began to thin, sending soft beams of moonlight onto the forest floor. Then Elanor saw it. The Mountain. The scent of it, of fire and iron and cedar and stone, now filled her senses. For a moment she lost herself in the wonderful smell. But not enough to miss the rustle of footsteps behind her.

Quickly she spun around, her knife finding the man's throat. Ioan grinned, his teeth gleaming in the light of the moon.

Chapter .2

"I could have killed you," Elanor said to her brother, quickly regretting how loudly her voice echoed. This was neither the time nor the place for conversation. She frowned and returned her knife to her belt.

Ioan's smile only deepened, showing all his dimples. He shared that grin with Rhys, who could only shake his head. Without another word, Ioan squeezed Elanor's arm, stepping out of the moonlight and back into darkness.

He wouldn't be the only person on guard tonight. At all times there were at least half a dozen well-armed Orphans protecting the expanse of land around the Mountain's entrance. Because even though they were inside the barrier,

6

even though it was past midnight, even though it was winter, the Orphans took no chances when it came to protecting their home.

The energy that had carried Elanor this far began to flag as she followed Rhys toward the Mountain's only point of entry. To the ignorant eye it might look like any other felled trunk, resting on the rock face at the edge of the forest. It looked like a dead end, nowhere to go but back. Elanor had once questioned the wisdom of living so close to Queen Josetta's palace, but it wasn't long before she realized that the Mountain's impenetrable sides and single, well-guarded entrance provided more strategic protection than any distance could offer them.

In the clearing between the Mountain and the forest, the stars and moon shimmered in the satin blue sky above them. The last leg of their journey revealed, they made their way toward the tree, its twisted roots facing them, spread like outstretched fingers. Elanor stepped inside the trunk, her hand finding the familiar ridges in the wood. Even though she knew that following the cuts on the wall would lead her inside the Mountain, to its warm, inviting glow, Elanor still hesitated before stepping into the complete blackness of the tunnel. She hated the dark.

But in she went. Twelve steps straight ahead and then

twenty-two down into the earth. When she reached the bottom, Elanor could see the faintest hint of illumination ahead. Two dozen steps more and then twenty up and into the light.

The entryway was quiet except for the soft echo of faraway water and the crackle of magic-lit candles melting into the rock ledges. Everything around her seemed to hum with magic, and the chill left her skin. For the first time in weeks, Elanor felt safe.

Carved into the entryway was an altar to honor the Four Sisters. Once upon a time, they had been legendary warriors who gave their lives in battle. As a reward for their bravery, they were allowed to remain in this life, but in different forms.

They had each thought carefully about what they would become. One of the sisters, known for her cunning, chose to become a fox. Another, known for her wisdom, asked to be an owl. The bravest of the sisters was transformed into a noble wolf, while the gentlest of the four became a swan.

Captured forever in stone, the Four Sisters were seated together, each wearing a mask that depicted the animal they had become. Each Orphan pledged loyalty toward one of the sisters. Kissing his fingers, Rhys touched the carving of Sister Swan and then brought his hand to his forehead. Elanor did the same to the statue of Sister Fox.

Behind the altar was a series of four tunnels. It was late, but Elanor knew Bronwyn would still be awake. She looked over at Rhys, who was doing his best to keep steady on his feet. In the candlelight she could see for the first time how truly exhausted he looked.

"You should have Dimia look at your head," she told him, though his bandage showed no signs of continued bleeding.

"Only after she looks at your shoulder."

In the excitement of returning home, Elanor had pushed aside her pain, but now it came roaring back, like an angry giant. She shook her head.

"I need to speak to Bronwyn," she said.

"I'll go with you."

"I can manage on my own," Elanor said firmly. "Go to the infirmary." When he hesitated, she drew herself up to her full height, still a head and a half shorter than he was. "Go see Dimia and then head immediately to the mineral pools. You stink."

Rhys smiled then, the expression softening the hard lines of weariness on his face. He bowed. "Yes, Your Majesty," he said.

Elanor watched him head straight down the tunnel where the infirmary and most of the sleeping quarters were. When he was out of sight, she gritted her teeth, adjusted her pack, and took the tunnel farthest to the right, toward the kitchen, dining cavern, and lodging for the Elders.

Elanor could hear an argument as she approached Bronwyn's quarters. She paused just beyond the threshold.

"You're being selfish," Wren was saying, her annoyance audible.

"I could say the same thing about you," Heck answered, calm as always.

Then Bronwyn called out. "It's rude to hover," she said. "Come in if you have something to say."

Her neck hot with embarrassment, Elanor pushed aside the curtain and entered. Wren was standing with her arms crossed, while Heck leaned casually on his crutches, one pant leg pinned neatly beneath his knee. The air was tense, the argument lingering in Wren's flushed face and Heck's frown. Only Bronwyn, seated in her chair, remained impassive, as usual.

"Next time you want to spy," she said, "avoid casting a shadow in my doorway."

"I didn't mean to eavesdrop," Elanor said.

Bronwyn waved Elanor's apology aside. "You've returned."

"Yes, Elder," Elanor said. Her pack was like a bag of rocks on her back, her feet and shoulder aching. "We came across a large party of huntsmen. Near the border of the Northern Kingdom."

"How close to the border?" Wren interrupted, her hand smoothing back short, brilliant-blond hair.

"Less than a day away."

"How large was the group?"

"Nearly a dozen," said Elanor. She didn't need to point out that this was more than double the usual size for one of Josetta's patrols.

"This is good news," said Heck.

Elanor was sure she had heard him wrong.

"You and I have a very different understanding of what good news looks like," Wren said, echoing Elanor's thoughts.

"If you would stop being stubborn and look at it from a different perspective, you might understand why I see it that way," Heck responded.

"I understand exactly why you see that way. I still think you're wrong," Wren snapped, glaring at him.

"What do you think it means?" Bronwyn stood, directing her question toward Elanor.

"That Josetta wants to expand her rule beyond the Midlands. Beyond the Western Kingdom."

"What would you recommend we do?"

Elanor was startled by the question. That was not

something she was usually asked. That was the job of Orphans like Wren and Heck, who were both several years older than Elanor and offered counsel to the Elders.

"I think we should find out how far the patrols are going," she said.

"It doesn't matter how far they're going," said Wren.

"It doesn't?" Heck asked, one dark eyebrow raised. "I think it matters quite a lot."

"It matters to you," she shot back.

"Both of you can leave," Bronwyn said abruptly. "I have heard what you have to say. I will discuss it with the other Elders."

Heck and Wren bowed their heads respectfully and made their exit, continuing their argument the moment the curtain fell behind them.

As their voices faded, Elanor turned back to Bronwyn, who had returned to her chair. Her twisted gray dreadlocks were up and circling her head, exposing a graceful neck scarred by age and war. Her hands were clasped in her lap, nearly disguising her missing fingers, two from her left hand and one from her right. She never referred to them, except once in a rare instance of humor, when she had joked that she should cut off one more to make it even. She had been drinking. No one had laughed.

"Did you at least retrieve the intended item?" Bronwyn asked. The Elders had not been pleased when they'd learned that four able-bodied rebels had intended to help one royal. But they had done nothing. Orphans were free to make their own decisions, something that set them apart not just from Josetta's followers but from other commoners who were at the mercy of royal commands.

"Rhys and I departed before the mission could be completed," Elanor said.

"I assume the others are still with the princess?" Bronwyn's disapproval was evident.

"Yes, Elder."

"We lost two Orphans during your absence," said Bronwyn. "Two more were injured."

If Bronwyn's intention was to make Elanor feel guilty, she had succeeded.

"Josetta's huntsmen targeted a village toward the south end of the kingdom. The royals had already abandoned it, leaving most of their servants behind. Most pledged loyalty to the Wicked Queen willingly."

"But not all," Elanor said, knowing exactly what came next.

"Not all. We attempted to help those who had been captured, hoping to free them before they were transported to the palace. The minute the huntsmen spotted us, they slaughtered their prisoners."

Elanor clenched her teeth. The treatment of disloyal commoners had become more and more vicious. "And the Queen?"

"What of the Queen?"

"Was she there?"

Bronwyn shook her head.

"It's been years," Elanor muttered to herself. The Orphans had not seen Josetta for many seasons. Wren argued that the Queen was surely present at each new acquisition of land or followers, most likely in disguise. Lately, however, even Wren was forced to admit that it was possible the Queen had not been outside her palace in some time. Her expansion into new territories, however, had accelerated.

"This concerns you?" Bronwyn asked.

"No," said Elanor quickly. "It's just—it's just unlike her." Josetta was a woman for whom control was of paramount importance.

"Unlike her? Do you feel you have an understanding of what is in her nature?"

The question wasn't meant to be cruel, but it still filled Elanor with shame.

"No, Elder," she said. "I don't understand the Wicked Queen at all."

Chapter .3

Three beds were occupied when Elanor finally made it to the infirmary. Two Orphans, presumably the ones injured in the failed rescue, were sleeping, as was Rhys, his head freshly bandaged and his face peaceful. At the other end of the room sat Dimia, her attention focused on her knitting needles, which were clacking pleasantly.

Tiny white spots had appeared behind Elanor's eyelids. How much blood had she lost? She removed her pack, careful not to jostle her shoulder. Instead of feeling relief when its weight was lifted, all of Elanor's injuries began to vie for her attention, each crying out in pain.

Knowing that Dimia had not heard her enter, Elanor

crossed the room, taking heavy steps. In the candlelight Elanor could see silvery strands snaking through Dimia's coarse black hair, matching the shimmering scarves draped across her shoulders. As Elanor moved into the healer's line of vision, Dimia's needles stilled and she glanced up.

"Elanor." Dimia smiled, putting aside her knitting. She stood, the happy expression dropping from her face as she noticed Elanor's blood-soaked jacket.

What happened? Dimia asked, signing. She could hear a little, but the healer often preferred communicating with her hands.

Arrow, Elanor responded with the often-used gesture.

Dimia *tsk*ed and motioned for Elanor to sit on one of the empty cots.

"Off," she ordered, pointing at Elanor's ruined clothes.

Elanor's shirt had not been removed since Rhys had pulled out the arrow several days ago. The scent of drying blood and dirt assailed her as she peeled off the layers of fabric covering her wound. She was filthy, her skin reeking of all the unwashed days between the Mountain and Muriel's, the last place she had been able to bathe.

"It's deep," Dimia said, cleaning away the dirt surrounding the open wound.

I've had worse, Elanor signed.

Once the injury was clean, the healer placed her palm over Elanor's shoulder and took a deep breath.

No one was more apt at healing than Dimia was. There was always less scarring, less recovery time. The warmth of magic filled the room, tickling Elanor's back before settling into her shoulder. In the space of a breath, the skin was stitched back together, leaving only a thin pink line.

It wasn't completely healed, of course. Magic, like all things, had limitations. The body could not be repaired so easily—it needed time to heal from the inside out, but at least it was protected now from any further damage or infection.

Was that the only one? Dimia signed, looking over the rest of Elanor's body.

Exhaustion had been hovering around Elanor like an unwelcome guest, and part of her wanted to nod so she could slip away and sleep, just as Rhys was doing. But she knew that ignoring her other injuries, even for a day, would do her no good.

Reluctantly she pointed at her feet.

Removing her shoes revealed that her feet were a mess. They were covered in sores; some red, shiny, and just about to burst; some bloody, worrying holes in her toes and soles.

Winter was hard on shoes, and Elanor had been trudging through the cold and the muck for too long. She had learned to ignore the pain while on patrol, the throbbing that came with each new blister and sore becoming part of her.

Dimia healed each wound, lancing some of them first. She then covered Elanor's feet with a salve of her own making, one that was cool and tingled pleasantly. It felt like magic in a jar, smooth and wonderful against Elanor's hot, aching skin.

Elanor wasn't the first to wear her feet bloody. She had no doubt that Rhys's feet looked somewhat similar, though he had probably gotten his shoes refitted before they left. He was always remembering to do things like that.

Looking enviously at him, Elanor considered for a moment stretching out onto one of the other cots and falling asleep. But her nose was full of her own stench, and she longed to scrub the weeks of forest away before she tumbled into her own bed, fresh and clean.

Come see me again tomorrow, Dimia signed as Elanor pulled on her filthy shirt and gathered up her broken shoes.

The mineral pools were empty. The air was thick and damp in this part of the Mountain. Two dozen glowing pools of still water spread across the cavern floor like enormous rain puddles. Stone paths wove between them, still wet with footprints. At one end of the cavern was a small waterfall, and the graceful splash the water made against the rocks reminded Elanor of a rainstorm in summer.

Unlike the rest of the Orphans' hideout, there were no candles lining the walls, yet the cavern was still bathed in light. The ceiling above was covered with millions of tiny, shimmering lights: glowworms, climbing up and down mossy garlands. The entire cavern was awash in gorgeous color, a perpetual blue twilight.

Elanor undressed and pulled her hair from its tight braid, rubbing her sore skull as she stepped under the warm water. She scrubbed until she was soft and clean, then grabbed fresh clothes from the line of laundry at the far end of the cave. The air wasn't as dense there, a cool breeze whispering into the cavern through a gap in the stone.

Her own room was cold, the fire in the forge unlit. But she was too tired to do anything but drop her bag near the door and head toward her bed. There were plenty of blankets to keep her warm tonight.

"Hello," she said to the fox curled up on her straw mattress. She ran a hand over the soft mottled fur and smiled.

Dagger blinked sleepily for a few seconds before recognizing her owner. She unwound herself and wiggled with an excitement that started at her beautiful full tail and ended at her wonderfully expressive nose. Elanor knelt next to the bed so the fox could sniff and lick her face; then she gathered the animal up in her arms. Elanor gave Dagger a gentle squeeze and received a friendly nip on her earlobe.

"You're getting a little heavy, aren't you?" Elanor said as she slid into bed, the fox cradled in her elbow. She tickled Dagger's stomach. "Someone's been very generous with scraps, haven't they? Or have you been begging?"

Dagger sniffed, as if insulted by the accusation, and maneuvered into her favorite position, curled against Elanor's neck. Suddenly the room wasn't cold anymore, and with her heartbeat matching Dagger's, Elanor closed her eyes and finally, finally slept.

Chapter .4

Elanor woke knowing someone was watching. Her knife was already in her hand. It always was. But she couldn't move. Something heavy and warm was draped across her neck.

"She's not the best guard," Tasmin said, and Elanor remembered where she was. She was in the Mountain. She was safe.

Turning her head, Elanor could see her adoptive mother through the soft fur on Dagger's tail. Then the hearty, wonderful scent of potatoes and onions floated toward her. Elanor's stomach growled as Tasmin held up a plate stacked high with fry cakes.

Elanor slipped her knife underneath her pillow, pushed

the sleeping fox off her neck, and sat up. Dagger grumbled in protest, but quickly settled onto the warm spot Elanor had vacated.

"Good morning," Tasmin said, extending the plate of food. Her sleeves were rolled to her elbows, revealing six black swans inked on her forearm. "I thought you might be hungry."

The fry cakes burned her fingers, but Elanor didn't care. She only noticed the perfect combination of potatoes and onions, mixed together in thin strips and fried until crispy. The outside was crunchy, the inside soft, all of it salty and hot and wonderful. Tasmin's cooking was what Elanor missed most when she was away from the Mountain, when she was eating nothing but dried meat and foraged fruit. It didn't take long for her to clean the plate. She felt full for the first time in weeks.

"I'm sorry I didn't come by last night," she said when she was done, but her mother waved a dismissive hand.

"I heard you spoke to Bronwyn," Tasmin said, sweeping her palm over the wood in the cold forge. The room crackled with magic and a fire roared to life. "Did something happen?"

Elanor nodded and explained what she and Rhys had seen.

"What did Bronwyn say?" Tasmin asked.

"She said she would talk to the other Elders. Heck and Wren were there. Heck said that this was a good sign."

"I'm sure Wren reacted to that well." Tasmin sighed, rubbing her forehead. "Has either of them approached you? No, I suppose you had already left before the conversation began."

"What conversation?"

Tasmin paused. Even though she was nearly the same age as Bronwyn, Tasmin had never once struck Elanor as old. But now, standing there, she suddenly looked ancient. Her brown skin, usually flushed from the warmth of the kitchen, seemed pallid and worn. Her gray hairs appeared to have multiplied, as had the wrinkles lining the corners of her eyes. She seemed exhausted.

"Heck is leaving," Tasmin said. "He's taking Hedra and whoever else he can convince, and he's leaving the Mountain."

Elanor was stunned. How was that possible? Like so many others, Heck had grown up in the Mountain. It was the place where Hedra, his daughter, had been born. His parents and wife had lived and died protecting the Mountain, and now he wanted to leave?

"No one will go with him," she said.

"Half a dozen plan to," Tasmin said quietly. "They'll leave at first melt."

"And where will they go?" Elanor couldn't believe Heck would do something so foolish. So selfish. "We need him here.

Josetta's power is growing. Soon she'll be crossing over into the Northern Kingdom."

"That's what Heck is counting on," said Tasmin, her voice calm and steady. "He believes that if Josetta attempts to take control of land in the North, the royals will fight back."

"What makes him think the Northerners won't just flee like the Westerners did?"

"The Western Kingdom was always weak, always poorly governed," Tasmin said. "I'm sure it's no coincidence that Josetta chose this kingdom as the place to begin her rule. But the North is strong. They will find a way to fight back."

As Tasmin spoke, her eyes regained some of their usual spark. She almost seemed hopeful.

"You think it's a good idea," Elanor realized with shock. "You want to go with him."

Tasmin reached out and took Elanor's hand. "I want *us* to go with him."

Elanor didn't understand what she was hearing. How could Tasmin even consider leaving the Mountain? She rarely ventured beyond the barrier, a spell she herself had created and controlled. It took immense concentration and skill to conjure magic powerful enough to hide an entire mountain, and every morning at dawn, Tasmin would wake and recast it. If she left, who would protect their home?

"No," Elanor said.

"I wish you would at least consider it."

"What about Ioan? Have you been trying to get him to leave as well?"

"Yes," Tasmin said. "And I'm not the only one."

"Heck has his own reasons for wanting Ioan to come with him."

"Far worse things have been done for love."

Elanor wrenched her hand from Tasmin's, not missing the hurt that crossed her mother's face. Guilt burned Elanor's throat, but she swallowed it, just as she always did.

"I can't leave," Elanor said. "Don't ask me again."

When Tasmin had gone, Elanor threw herself down on the floor and began to work her muscles. At first her body resisted, but after a while the pain began to feel good. It felt substantial. Her arms burned, her heart pounding in her ears.

Elanor loved her body. She loved the muscles in her arms and her legs. She loved the thickness of her thighs and the width of her shoulders. She loved that she could climb a tree faster than anyone else and on a good day nearly outrun Dagger. She loved that her stomach had a softness to it, a roundness owed to Tasmin's food.

She loved her hair, long and thick, flat against her skull.

She loved the weight of it against her shoulder blades. She loved her hands, small and rough, broken nails and perfect aim. She loved what her body could do. It was strong, it was soft, and it was capable.

The roots of her hair were damp with sweat, but Elanor clenched her teeth and pushed herself again and again and again. She just needed to stop thinking.

She had nearly succeeded when Rhys found her.

"Wren is putting together a raiding party," he said, looking well rested. "Are you in?"

"Of course." Her clothes were soaked, but she didn't care. Quickly she braided her hair and gathered her weapons. There were no mirrors in the Mountain, but she could still remember her reflection in the Queen's looking glass. Eyes sharp as blades, hair black as steel. Skin pale as ash, with constellations of freckles, and lips she often bit until they bled.

"I won't be long," she told Dagger, who had snuggled back into the unmade bed. The fox yawned and peered up at Elanor, as if she understood.

With knives strapped to her thighs, an ax at her waist, and her bow and arrows slung over her uninjured shoulder, Elanor followed Rhys through the tunnel. As they walked she told him about Heck's plan.

"He's no good to us if he doesn't want to be here," Rhys

said, shrugging. Nothing ever worried him. As he had once told Elanor, as long as he had his good looks and his good arm, everything else would work out. Elanor never bothered to correct him about the "good arm" part—he had a tendency to aim too far to his left, but even she couldn't deny his good looks. With his charmingly crooked nose, easy smile, and warm brown skin, he was quite pleasant to look at. There wasn't a single person in the Mountain who hadn't been in love with Rhys at some point or another.

A group of a dozen or so Orphans were gathered in the dining hall, all eyes on Wren. Gideon was at her side as usual. The two of them were an impressive sight, both wearing leather harnesses that crisscrossed their chests and displayed an extensive array of knives. Their arms were bare, revealing muscled biceps decorated with intricate tattoos snaking from wrist to the shoulder.

"We'll head out soon," Wren said. "The caravan crossed the border into the Midlands early this morning. There are half a dozen guards, but they are older and slow." Wren's knowledge of these strangers wasn't a surprise. A bird couldn't build a nest in the Midlands without her knowing about it. "Gather your weapons, some breakfast, and we'll meet at the altar shortly."

Elanor was still hungry and grabbed several more fry

cakes from the center of the table. They were cold but still good. Between bites, she noticed that Wren was standing nearby, peeling an apple with one of her many knives, keeping the skin in one long curl.

Despite the collection of beautiful images decorating Wren's arms, Elanor's eyes went immediately to the red lines just barely visible around her wrists. The only markings that had been added to her body without permission.

Wren had lived within Josetta's walls nearly as long as Elanor had. But Wren had been used, not as a servant, but as an experiment. The lines around her wrists were a permanent reminder of what the Queen had done to her.

Josetta believed that she was saving them from themselves. That she was helping them. It wasn't until Elanor had been rescued that the Orphans realized exactly what the Queen had accomplished.

It was Tasmin who had discovered what had happened. And it was Tasmin who had to explain to Elanor why she was different from most of the other women in the Mountain. Why she could barely feel the magic inside of her, let alone use it instinctively.

"Magic is water," Tasmin had said. "It's a well inside of each woman. Sometimes the bucket is easy to fill, easy to draw. Sometimes it's hard. And sometimes"—Tasmin had taken

Elanor's hand—"sometimes the rope is damaged."

The Queen had weakened the rope that connected Elanor to her magic. But for Wren it had been severed.

Her apple completely peeled, Wren stared at Elanor and crossed her arms over her chest. Quickly Elanor looked away. Guilt burned her tongue.

"We should go," said Gideon, looking up from the knife he had been polishing.

Finally breaking eye contact with Elanor, Wren glanced over at him and nodded. "Let's move out," she said.

They stopped in the entryway, in front of the altar. At the foot of it was a bowl of cinders, which the Orphans dipped their hands into, smearing their faces with soot. It made Elanor feel invisible and safe. There was the snap of magic as one of the Orphans lit the candle in each sister's hand, moving aside so that Wren could lay a sword at their feet.

"Sisters," Wren said, her voice loud and clear. "May you bless us with strength, cunning, loyalty, and grace. May we exit each battle with the same bravery with which we entered. May you guide us in this life and the next." She turned to the group and raised her weapon. "Happy hunting!"

"Happy hunting!" everyone repeated, voices booming in the confined space.

Outside the air was cold and crisp. Elanor buttoned

her coat to her neck and pulled her hood over her head. She could see her breath, white clouds that disappeared almost immediately.

"Smells like snow." Ioan caught up to her as they moved through the forest. His voice was low, barely a whisper, his teeth bright amidst the charcoal disguising his face.

If one were to look at them quickly, one might assume that they were blood siblings, as they shared narrow, heavy-lidded eyes and iron-black hair.

But Ioan was six years older and big, with a barrel chest and thick waist. His face was round and prone to smiling, and his skin always seemed a little flushed. Everything about him was relaxed, from his graceful way of walking to his languid fighting style. Elanor was compact. Controlled. She was small and sturdy, with wide shoulders and strong legs. Neither of them looked anything like Tasmin.

Elanor loved Ioan as if he was her real brother. Which meant that while she always loved him, sometimes she didn't like him very much. Was he truly thinking of leaving the Mountain with Heck?

"It's only a few days away," Elanor muttered back, looking up at the sky. The world right before the first snowfall always looked so barren, so lifeless. She felt exposed in the forest at this time of year, unprotected in the emptiness.

They both quieted as they passed through the barrier, magic dancing across their skin. One could never be too safe in the forest.

The Orphans spread out as they headed toward the road, weapons drawn. Elanor kept her eyes and ears alert, her gaze darting through the trees in front of her while she strained to hear anything other than the soft footsteps of those around her. Though the Queen's huntsmen were not known for their stealth, it was always best to be on constant alert.

They walked for several hours, none of them speaking. Then through the trees, Elanor spotted the break in the forest where the road was, hearing the rumble of horse hooves and carriage wheels coming their way. Wren had planned the ambush well.

The Orphans hid, taking shelter behind the wide trunks of the trees that crowded the side of the road. Keeping her eyes on Wren, Elanor waited, her back pressed against the rough bark. When she saw the signal, she pulled her handkerchief up beneath her eyes and notched an arrow to her bow.

Chapter .5

It was a large traveling party. There was a carriage and almost two dozen soldiers on horseback flanking it. As the party passed, Elanor could see why Wren had targeted them. The guards wore heavy chain mail and large helmets that covered their faces, making it hard for them to see and move quickly. They were as effective as golden eggs up on their horses.

Elanor didn't recognize the crest on their chests, and their armor was unfamiliar. It looked old and out-of-date. And even though it was polished, she spotted a hint of rust here and there. Clearly it had been neglected for some time. Elanor eyed the carriage as it rolled down the road. The roof was loaded with sacks and trunks. She hoped it was full of useful items like flour and grain.

Up ahead, she saw Wren give the signal.

Elanor and the others crept out from the safety of the forest, weapons drawn.

"Halt!" Wren's voice was slightly muffled by her disguise, but still loud enough to cause the carriage to come to an immediate stop. "Put your hands up."

Immediately the soldiers reached for their swords, armor clanking with every movement. There was a whistle of an arrow, and one of the horses gave a loud whinny. It reared up, dumping its rider to the ground.

"Try that again and the next arrow will be buried between *your* legs, not your horse's," Wren warned. "Hands up!"

Every single hand shot into the air.

"Now place them behind your necks, fingers laced!" she yelled. "We have no desire to hurt you, but don't give us an excuse."

Elanor kept her drawn bow aimed at the carriage while Ioan and the others began unloading it and unburdening some of the soldiers of their weapons.

"Don't worry, lad," Elanor heard Rhys say to one of them. "It's your weapon I'm after, not your virtue."

Even from her position, Elanor could see why Rhys had

gone for the small dagger first. It was a beautiful item, with a curved blade and a handle decorated in gems.

It didn't take long to unload the carriage, and most of the Orphans fled quickly through the trees, those with the heaviest burdens departing first. They would head straight to the Mountain. Elanor remained, her arrow trained on the soldiers.

"I wouldn't recommend following us," Wren finally said, retrieving the arrow she had shot, indicating for Elanor and the other archers to head back into the forest. "We're faster than you, and it's quite clear our reflexes are better."

And with that they were off, dashing through the woods, keeping their eyes in front of them, ears listening for the sounds of a pursuit. Elanor doubted they would try—the Orphans had taken most of the weapons, and the horses would be useless in the dense trees, but still they didn't stop running until they were at least a mile from the road.

Breathing heavily, she returned her arrow to her pack and rubbed at her sore shoulder. Her feet, still tender, throbbed in her too-stiff shoes. Around her the others gathered, catching their breath. She spotted Rhys carefully examining the dagger he had taken from the soldier. He caught her watching and raised it triumphantly. Clearly he had decided which item he was claiming.

It was a good knife, Elanor could see that as she walked over to him. It was likely that he had been distracted by the white and blue gems decorating the handle, but it was also a beautifully made weapon. As was the scabbard it came in. She reached out and traced the leather. Soft, old. Like all good leather, it had only become better with age. It clearly had been made for the dagger, which was an unusual size. Smaller than most, it had a dangerously curved blade. Deadly, if used correctly.

Ioan sidled up to them.

"Where do you think they were headed?" he asked, his voice low. The others were disappearing into the forest. It was time to head home.

Elanor shrugged. It didn't matter much to her—the caravan was going to arrive empty-handed no matter their planned destination. Then she caught a glance at Ioan's face, at his flushed cheeks, and her stomach twisted.

She knew that look. The robbery had gone smoothly, which meant that Ioan was bored. He was reckless when he was bored. He wiggled his eyebrows at her, but Elanor shook her head. She wasn't going to be a part of his foolishness. Ioan turned to Rhys.

"Feel like an adventure?"

The two of them were the worst kind of influence on each other.

Rhys grinned. "Always."

There was nothing Elanor could do but watch them take off into the woods, in the direction they had just come from.

The loot had been spread out and the others were just beginning to claim their rewards when Elanor returned to the Mountain. It was a good haul, with several sacks of flour and sugar, which would be greatly appreciated by those in the kitchen. Those items were hardest to come by every winter.

Elanor took a seat and observed the frenzy. She would sort through whatever was left. Most of the Orphans went for the items that looked the most impressive, which were not often the ones best suited for them.

Wren dropped into the chair next to her. "Pick the ones you'd like to use for scrap," she said with a big smile, her good mood evident.

"How's your arrow supply?" Elanor asked. It had been a long while since she'd had time to make anything new. An afternoon of melting down steel and repurposing it sounded wonderful.

Wren swung her feet up onto the table, her hands testing the weight and balance of one of the stolen swords. "Decent. We didn't lose any today, but I'd always prefer to have more than we need."

Nodding, Elanor stood and began to sift through the remaining weapons, picking out the more poorly made items. Like the armor on the soldiers, most of the swords seemed somewhat old-fashioned, with hints of rust near the handles. She frowned. It didn't take much effort to care for a weapon. Luckily for her, there were almost a dozen items that she could melt down and remake into something more useful.

"I'll take these," she said, carefully gathering them up.

"How long will you need?" Wren asked, pulling an ax off the table.

"Few days," Elanor said, already thinking of what she could make with them. "How do you feel about broadheads?" she asked.

"Broadheads are a nasty business," Wren commented.

"War is a nasty business."

"It is indeed," Wren said with a grin.

There was a lot of steel. Elanor could make simple arrowheads, of course, but those were easy. She felt like a challenge. That knife that Rhys had chosen, that beautiful curved blade. Elanor wondered if she could make one like it. Her mind began whirling like a spinning wheel, filled with possibilities.

♡ ♡ ♡

The metal was red hot. Fire blazing in the forge, Elanor wiped the sweat from her brow, the rough gloves scratching her skin. But she barely noticed. All she could see were flames and steel as she watched what had been a nicked and uncared-for sword transform into a smooth, shimmering liquid. It was beautiful and hypnotic, the slide of melted metal into broadhead molds, the fire's heat burning against her cheeks and nose. She had been working for hours, but it was exactly what she needed. It was focused, careful work that required all her concentration. There was nothing more dangerous than working with fire if your mind was elsewhere, and she had the scars and burns to prove it. But she wasn't distracted now. All other thoughts had been pushed aside, her attention directed to the task at hand.

Then her stomach growled. She had been avoiding Tasmin since their argument this morning, but after missing lunch, it would not do for her to skip another meal out of spite. Dagger was fast asleep on the still-unmade bed, so Elanor left the fox undisturbed and the steel cooling next to the forge and went to find something remaining from dinner.

She was heading down the tunnel when she heard a clatter in the entryway. She drew her ax and ran toward the sound, stopping abruptly when she saw Rhys kneeling in front of the altar of the Four Sisters. Some soot was still smeared across his cheeks, but he was soaked with sweat as he gripped Sister Swan's stone knee, trying to pray while still gasping for breath.

"Sister Swan," he choked, "please help me."

"Rhys!" Elanor slid to the floor next to him.

"Ellie!" His eyes were wide, his skin flushed.

"What happened?" she asked.

His face crumpled like wet parchment. "You need to help me," he said. "Ioan's been captured."

Chapter .6

Elanor's fingers were wrapped tightly around her ax. The moon was a milky eye above the barren treetops, but she could barely make out Rhys ahead of her. He was setting a brutal pace, and Elanor struggled to keep up.

The cold air slapped her face as she pushed forward, trying to keep her steps light and quick, even though she knew that anyone out in the forest would no doubt hear Rhys plowing through the dead leaves and branches. It wasn't stealth that was needed, it was speed. She could only hope that there were no huntsmen out in the woods tonight.

"They took him," he had said to her, kneeling in front

of the altar, his voice rough. "I didn't know what to do." He hung his head. "So I ran."

"Tell me what happened."

"We followed the carriage. It went to the palace."

Elanor's mouth had gone dry, but she remained silent.

"I should have been more careful." Rhys had closed his eyes, his face a mixture of shame and frustration. "We were so busy watching the carriage, we didn't even see the huntsmen."

"They caught you," Elanor finished dully.

Rhys had nodded. "I managed to get away. I don't know how, but I did and—" His voice faltered. "And I ran."

Ioan had always been the lucky one. His face had never been included in Josetta's wanted posters. He had never been captured by the Queen and had never spent time within her castle walls. Like Rhys, he had escaped as a child and had never been branded. Now it seemed his luck had run out.

"We'll use the tunnel," Elanor had said, hoping that Ioan would remember what to do.

The tunnel had been dug by his parents. It had been created to rescue several of the children who *had* been stolen, but it had been used very rarely since the death of Ioan's parents almost ten years ago. The tunnel led straight to Josetta's dungeons. All Orphans knew that if they were captured by the Queen, their only chance for escape was dependent on getting themselves thrown in prison, where there was the possibility of being rescued.

Trying to get beyond the dungeons, however, was suicide, as had been proven over the past few years by several ambitious Orphans hoping to kill the Queen in her own bed. Elanor could only pray that her brother had been thrown into a cell and not immediately executed.

It took nearly all night for Elanor and Rhys to reach the palace. Generations ago, before Elanor had been born, thorn bushes had been planted less than a quarter mile from the outer wall, one more obstacle to overcome. It had been a long time since anyone had attempted to bypass them, and while there were broken vines to indicate where they had hacked apart the thick brambles, Elanor and Rhys still had to clear a new path.

The sharp thorns caught on Elanor's sleeves as she cut a narrow swath through the nature-made barrier. Creating too large a hole in the briar wall could put them all at risk. It couldn't be obvious where they had entered. Better to get pricked than to get caught, as Bronwyn always said. Brambles were common in this part of the woods.

Ignoring the stinging cuts on her hands, Elanor followed Rhys to the base of the palace. It had been built along a hill, and the tunnel had been dug through the dirt and into the prison. With the first light of day illuminating her search, Elanor smoothed her palm across the barren slope until she found a rough slab of wood. Pulling it aside revealed a hole barely large enough for one person to crawl through. It was so dark. Doing her best to hide a shudder, she moved aside so Rhys might get a better look.

He reached inside and patted the dirt. "Feels firm," he said.

"Let's hope the rest of the tunnel held up as well as the entrance," said Elanor. Neither of them had ever attempted a rescue like this. It had been a long time since an Orphan had been caught by the Queen and her huntsmen. Elanor clenched and unclenched her fists, as if that would make her less anxious.

Rhys removed his bow and arrows and handed them to her. They would be too unwieldy to take into the tunnel, especially for someone of his size. He would have to make do with his daggers.

"I'll see you soon," Rhys said, squeezing her arm.

"Good hunting," she said, watching him fold his lanky body through the small entrance. For a moment it seemed as though he wouldn't fit, his back and shoulders dragging through the dirt. But somehow he managed and, crawling slowly, eventually disappeared into the tunnel. Shouldering his bow, Elanor stepped away from the wall and out of the light of the rising sun.

It didn't take her long to shimmy up one of the nearby trees, one that took her above the top of the briar wall. From there she had a good view of both the tunnel and the land around it. She would be able to see anyone coming. Rhys had until midday. That was the rule.

Even though they both knew she would have fit better, Elanor was grateful that he hadn't suggested she be the one to go. But he knew better than that. He knew she wasn't going inside those walls again.

Like Ioan, Rhys was one of the few in their generation unbranded by Josetta. Ioan and his family had been the first to discover the Mountain and take shelter there, while Rhys's parents had managed to hide him in a tree stump just before they were attacked and killed by Josetta's huntsmen—men and women who had not long before been their neighbors and friends. Rhys was taken back to the Mountain and raised alongside Ioan and the other rescued children. Most of them had grown up together.

It was years before Elanor was brought to the Mountain, and all she remembered of her life before that was what she had experienced on the other end of that tunnel. The prison had been dark and wet and smelled terrible. There had been many children, all taken from their parents and thrown together in one cell. Brigid and Thackery had been there. And Wren. Wren had been the oldest.

Elanor had been very young, and everything before that time was hazy—the faces of her parents, her childhood home—but the prison she remembered well. It was as if her life had started there, the rest of it neatly erased.

They had been left in the cell for several days, all of them huddled together for warmth. Every so often there would be a whimper or wail, each child crying private tears. Except Wren. Elanor never saw her cry. Because of that they all trusted her. Her bravery made it bearable.

At some point—hours, maybe days later—they were led to a courtyard. The sunlight burned Elanor's eyes as she was placed in a line with the others. It was the first time she saw Josetta.

Dressed in a scarlet gown, the Queen regarded them all. Across her shoulders was a fur cloak, made of perfect orange foxtails. A gold crown lay against her forehead, nestled in the mass of red curls that settled around her face like a fiery cloud. Her features were pale and sharp, her lips crimson and her eyes green.

She walked up and down the line of children. Elanor could remember feeling ashamed that she was so filthy, curling her hands into fists when Josetta approached, for she could see the Queen's perfectly shaped, perfectly clean nails.

Some of the others began to cry, and Josetta stopped. Out

of the corner of her eye, Elanor saw Josetta raise a silk-clothed arm and point to those who were weeping.

"Kitchen!" she'd said. "Since they're already teary, make them chop all the onions in the castle."

The children were taken away, their wailing escalating as they were pulled apart from the others. The bigger kids, like Thackery, were taken next. "Barracks," the Queen had ordered. "Give them a meal and a bed, start training them tomorrow."

One by one the children were given a place and a task. It grew quiet.

Elanor had kept her eyes on the ground. Was everyone gone? Was she alone? She was just about to risk a glance when the hem of the red dress, sparkling in the sunlight, appeared in her line of sight.

"Look at me," Josetta demanded.

Elanor raised her head. The Queen's green eyes searched her face. She glanced to the left and right of Elanor, where several girls still remained, Wren included.

"She'll do." Josetta snapped her fingers. "Bathe her, dress her, and take her to my chamber. The others . . ." She paused. "They go to my private study."

It was many years before Elanor learned what happened in Josetta's private study, but at that moment she only knew she was being taken away, and it was only the huntsmen with their sharp swords that kept her from throwing herself on the ground and begging to remain with the others. And even though she kept her mouth shut, Elanor could not stop the tears from rolling, hot and fast, down her dirty cheeks.

"I won't have any crying," Josetta had said. "You're lucky. Don't be ungrateful."

Suddenly someone toppled out of the tunnel.

He wasn't as tall as Rhys, he wasn't as wide as Ioan, and he let out a cry as he somersaulted onto the ground, ending up on his back. Elanor scrambled down the tree, feeling dangerously exposed in the early morning sun. She approached, ax extended, but the stranger didn't move from his prone position on the forest floor.

There was a gash on his forehead, the blood already beginning to dry. His hair was matted and dirty, the pale red curls contrasting with his dark skin. There was a bruise just to the left of his wide nose and another mark forming on his square jaw. Though his clothes were ripped and filthy, Elanor could still tell that they were expensive and well made, his shirt hemmed with shimmering gold thread and his trousers tailored to fit him. Elanor nudged him with her foot and he let out a soft moan. His pale eyelashes fluttered and then finally parted.

"Hello?" His eyes were brown.

"Who are you?" Elanor asked, her weapon at the ready.

But there wasn't any time for him to answer, because Ioan came crawling out of the tunnel, his face contorted in pain. He toppled onto the ground next to the stranger, his clothes smeared with dirt. But when he landed on his back, he cried out and curled into himself. As he clutched his knees, Elanor saw that the back of his shirt was covered in blood. She dropped to the earth next to him.

"Ioan!" She placed a careful hand on his arm.

He blinked up at her. "Ellie?" he asked, his eyes full of pain and then recognition. "Ellie."

"We need to go!" Rhys crawled out of the tunnel only slightly more gracefully than the others, quickly covering the entrance.

"What happened?" Elanor asked as Rhys helped her pull Ioan to his feet. He was as heavy as a sack of rocks.

Rhys looked at her. "They branded him," he said.

Stomach contracting, Elanor took a deep breath. "Can you walk?" she asked her brother.

The nod he gave was listless, but he seemed able to support himself on his feet.

"I'll help him," Rhys said, looping one of Ioan's arms over his shoulder.

The stranger was still lying on the ground, his eyes closed again. "Who is he?" Elanor asked.

"He was in the cell with Ioan," Rhys said. "I couldn't just leave him."

Suddenly the stranger groaned and abruptly sat up. His hand flew to his forehead, and his face went ashen. Still, he struggled to his feet.

"My—my friends," he said, gesturing toward the tunnel.

He took a step in that direction but tripped. Elanor grabbed him before he could fall. She wrapped her arm around his waist, bracing against his weight, most of which he was unable to support on his own.

"I need to help my friends," he said, his words slurring just slightly.

"You're in no shape to help anyone," Rhys said, exchanging a look with Elanor. It was a look that asked, *What do we do?*

Elanor didn't know. It was clear that this stranger needed a healer, but they had Ioan to take care of, and transporting both of them would add extra time to their trip back to the Mountain. A trip that was dangerous enough already. Ioan's injuries were not life threatening, but Elanor knew that if they left this young man behind, he would surely die.

"What's your name?" she asked.

"My name?" The stranger squinted at her.

"Your name," Rhys repeated.

"M-Matthias," he finally said, though it seemed to take great effort.

"Well, Matthias," Elanor said, wrapping his arm over her shoulder. "I'm Elanor." He was far taller than she was but sagging an awful lot. She could feel ribs beneath the thin shirt he wore. He was shivering, but his clothes were soaked with sweat.

"Elanor," Matthias repeated dumbly. "You're strong."

"I know," she said.

"My friends," he said again. "I need to help them."

"You can't help them like this, mate," Rhys said, his arm around Ioan, who seemed to be making a great effort to focus on the situation at hand, his face still twisted in pain. "You're the one who needs help."

Matthias looked down at Elanor. Even though he wasn't smiling, she could still see the crease of a dimple at the corner of his mouth.

"We need to go," she said. "Come on." Elanor tightened her grip on his waist and began to pull him in the direction of the Mountain.

Chapter 7

It was a slow journey. Ioan was walking better on his own but kept stumbling, and while Matthias was doing his best to support his own weight, Elanor found that she was doing most of the work as the sun began to set. They had made the trek in silence—it was risky enough traveling during daylight, but they didn't have much of a choice with two of them injured. So far they had been exceptionally lucky.

There had been no sign of huntsmen patrolling the area, which only added to Elanor's suspicion that Josetta's attentions were focused elsewhere. Had she sent most of her army toward the border? Was she truly brash enough to attempt to take land in the Northern Kingdom?

As the stars began to appear in the sky, Elanor heard Rhys and Ioan talking up ahead, their voices hushed and urgent. She could barely see them in the dark.

"You should have told me," Elanor heard Rhys whisper.

"You would have left him there," Ioan argued.

"This is not the time nor the place for conversation," Elanor hissed at both of them.

Rhys had drawn his sword. "Matthias was part of the caravan we robbed. The one that went directly to the palace."

Immediately Elanor's arm fell from the stranger's waist and she twisted away, her ax going to his throat.

"Wait!" Ioan said, grabbing her arm.

She roughly shook him off. "Who are you?" Elanor demanded, the blade against Matthias's neck. "Are you one of Josetta's men?"

"No!" he said, hands raised. "No. We were captured! We were thrown in the dungeon!"

"Why were you there?" Rhys pressed.

"I don't know!" Matthias said, his eyes wide. "We were sent there."

"Why would Josetta put him in prison if he was one of hers?" Ioan asked.

"Stay out of this," Elanor snapped, but Ioan didn't back down.

"He protected me," he said. "That's how he got injured. I swear on the Four Sisters." Ioan placed his fingers on his forehead. "Please, Ellie, he needs our help. We can decide what to do with him later, but right now he needs help."

Elanor could see that Matthias was fading fast. He was sweating and shivering at the same time, his skin a grayish hue. Sucking in a breath, Elanor took her knife and sliced off the bottom inch or so of the shirt she wore beneath her jacket. She handed it to Ioan.

"He'll need to go the rest of the way blindfolded," she said. "And he's your responsibility." Then she turned and stalked off in the direction of the Mountain.

A frigid breeze whipped through Elanor, cutting her to the bone. Her fingers, wrapped protectively around her ax, were so cold that they hurt, and she had lost feeling in her nose and ears several miles back. Behind her the footsteps of the others had stopped. Elanor whipped around to discover the two Orphans staring up. Even Matthias, who was still blindfolded, had tilted his face upward.

Snow was drifting down from the cloud-covered sky, barely illuminated by the glow of the hidden moon. Icy white flakes swirled in the cold air, coming to rest on Elanor's cheeks and eyelashes, soft as a kiss. Taking a deep breath, she filled her lungs with the sharp, crisp scent of winter.

The snow was coming down fast, blanketing the forest floor as they continued on their way. Elanor noticed that both Rhys and Ioan were supporting Matthias, who seemed to be struggling to stay conscious. She could hear Ioan muttering encouragement, though the labored sound of his voice indicated that he was supporting a great deal of weight.

All of a sudden the air around them crackled. They had passed the barrier.

Tasmin's spell was a powerful one. Those in the Mountain, who had pledged their allegiance to the Orphans, were immune, as were those they brought through the barrier. But anyone else who came through, either accidentally or by design, was hit with dizzying confusion. Usually trespassers turned around and headed back in the direction they'd come from, but even those who continued on were distracted, vulnerable, and easily caught by Orphans on guard. In the past ten years, no one had ever discovered the entrance to the Mountain. Elanor planned on keeping it that way.

Elanor heard a retching noise and turned to find Matthias emptying his last meal onto the forest floor. He was getting worse.

Rhys seemed to draw the same conclusion. "We should get him to Dimia immediately," he said. "His head looks bad."

"Go get Bronwyn," she told him. "Ioan and I will take him to the infirmary." An Elder needed to be alerted about the presence of a stranger immediately. Rhys nodded and took off through the trees.

"Let's hurry," she said to Ioan. If she held on to the stranger's waist, she could keep him upright while Ioan managed to propel him forward. She could feel Matthias's feverish skin through his ripped clothes.

Navigating the entrance, through the fallen tree trunk and down and up the stairs into the Mountain, wasn't easy, but Matthias seemed to be making a valiant effort to assist them. The blindfold had fallen off at some point, but his eyes remained closed.

Dimia was waiting for them, a clean sheet spread across one of the cots. She gestured for them to lay him down.

What happened? she signed.

He hit his head on a wall, Ioan explained, pointing to the gash on Matthias's forehead. There was a large lump, too, which probably meant he had cracked his skull pretty hard.

Dimia carefully examined the injury. *He needs the slumber,* she signed.

"Wait!" Wren pulled back the infirmary's curtain, stepping aside to let Bronwyn pass. Rhys was right behind them.

Bronwyn approached the cot.

"Give her your hands," Wren told Matthias. "Now!" she demanded when he hesitated.

Arms trembling, Matthias put his palms on Bronwyn's. Immediately a pulse of magic surrounded them.

"Do you wish harm on anyone in the Mountain?" Wren took charge of the questioning.

"N-no," Matthias said.

"Are you one of Josetta's huntsmen?" Wren asked.

"No."

"Do you pledge loyalty to her?"

"No." This answer came without hesitation.

Wren looked at Bronwyn, whose eyes had been closed during the entire exchange, and Elanor held her breath.

"He's not lying," Bronwyn finally said. Dropping Matthias's hands, she stepped back. "You may put him in the slumber now. He can hardly do us any damage if he's unconscious," she said before leaving the room.

Elanor signed the Elder's orders to Dimia, who nodded. As the healer turned to gather supplies, Matthias grabbed Elanor's hand. His grip was surprisingly strong, his fingers soft.

"What is happening?" he asked. There was fear in his eyes.

"Dimia is going to take care of you," she said.

Still he held on tight. "What is she going to do?" His voice was scared and small.

"They're going to put you in the slumber," Ioan said. "Your body needs to heal."

"The slumber?"

"You'll be fine." Ioan took his other hand. Only then did Matthias's grip on Elanor relax.

She stepped back, away from the cot, away from Matthias. Pressing herself against the cold stone of the wall, she kept her gaze down. The slumber made her uneasy. It was a powerful spell, only used by the most accomplished healers. Most injuries could be healed with magic, repaired from the outside, and time would do the rest. But there were some that required complete quiet and immobility. Injuries that could be fatal if the healing process were disturbed. So the severely wounded were put into the slumber, a deep sleep that they could not wake from on their own.

But that sleep was not always a peaceful one. It could be unnerving, filled with twisted dreams and nightmares. Elanor's hand went to her neck, to the raised scar that curved over her shoulder. After she had been woken from the slumber, it had been weeks before she stopped being afraid of closing her eyes. Years later she still feared the dark.

But sometimes it was not enough to save a life. The first girl Elanor had loved had been brought out of the slumber only so that she could say good-bye. But she had woken in pain, crying out for her mother, a woman who had died just after giving her life, someone who she had never known. Elanor had tried to hold her hand. Had tried to calm her, had tried to make her focus, to make her understand what was happening, but all she could do was scream. There were times that Elanor still heard those screams.

"He's asleep," Rhys said, joining her against the wall.

Elanor glanced up. Dimia was in front of the cot, but she could see Matthias's boots, limply pointed outward. As the healer stepped away, Elanor saw that the wound on his head had been bandaged, the cut on his lip healed, and the bruises on his cheek were already beginning to fade. He looked peaceful, his face relaxed and still, but those in the slumber always looked peaceful. Beneath his eyelids, she could see his eyes moving, and she hoped that his dreams were calm and familiar. She did not wish fear on anyone.

Next to him, Ioan sat on another one of the cots, slowly unbuttoning his shirt. Dimia waited patiently as he peeled the fabric away, his face twisted in pain.

Elanor bit the inside of her mouth as the brand was uncovered. It had been a while since she had seen one so fresh, but it was just as terrible as she remembered. Her brother's skin was red and raised around the blackened mark. Josetta had chosen Ioan to be a stable hand, as indicated by the crude horseshoe now permanently displayed on his shoulder.

Ioan caught her gaze. He squared his jaw and smiled. "I've always wanted an excuse to visit Gideon," he said. It was Gideon's ink that most Orphans used to disguise Josetta's work.

Elanor's shoulder itched, as if her brand was exposed.

Wren crossed her own decorated arms.

"Did you learn anything?" she asked.

Ioan shook his head, wincing as Dimia cleaned the wound. "They forced me to keep my head down. I didn't see a thing."

"Did they suspect you were an Orphan?"

"I think I convinced them I was stupid and lost."

"Probably wasn't that difficult," Rhys muttered to Elanor.

Ioan shot a look at his friend and continued. "They made me get on my knees in the center of the courtyard, and a man said I'd be perfect for the stables. That's when they did"—he nodded back toward his shoulder—"this."

"That can't be right," Elanor protested. "Josetta is the one who makes those decisions. Are you sure it wasn't her?" She couldn't imagine the Queen ever allowing someone else to take on that responsibility.

"I can tell the difference between a man's voice and a woman's, Ellie," Ioan said. "Besides, does it really matter who picked the brand today? We all know who created them."

But it did matter. At least it did to Elanor. It was just one more unusual thing to worry about.

"How'd you get them to put you in the dungeon? Why didn't they just take you to the stables?" Wren asked.

"I bit one of the guards," Ioan said, somewhat proudly. "So they threw me into the cell."

"With him." Wren gestured toward a prone Matthias.

Ioan nodded. "The guards shoved me in with him. They were going to beat me, but Matthias jumped in front of them, and that's how he was injured."

"How long do you think it will be before they notice you're gone?" Wren asked.

"They didn't seem to be very concerned with counting their prisoners. I didn't see another guard," Ioan said. "But I couldn't say for sure."

"Matthias said his friends were there, as well," Rhys added. "He wanted to go back and rescue them."

"The rest of the caravan," Wren said, looking thoughtful. "Something to discuss with him when he comes out of the slumber."

Suddenly Heck came stumbling through the curtains, his

eyes searching the room frantically before settling on Ioan. Those same eyes quickly narrowed and shifted to Wren, who looked thoroughly uninterested in Heck's appearance.

"I heard there was an attack," he said, leaning heavily on his crutches as he struggled to hide his concern.

"Not quite." Wren looked down at her nails. "Ioan got himself captured; Rhys and Elanor rescued him and brought us a prisoner of our own. Nothing to worry yourself with."

Heck glanced at Matthias.

"We already interrogated him," Wren said, as if reading his mind.

"You should have included me." Heck's face was flushed, his neck red.

"I didn't see the point," Wren said. "You'll be leaving at first melt. The sooner we start making decisions without you, the better."

"I should still be informed when one of our own—" Heck was looking everywhere but at Ioan. "When one of our own is taken."

Ioan was also looking away, his attention focused on his hands. The tension in the room was as dense as a briar thicket.

"Ioan was taken. He has now been returned," said Wren. "Consider yourself informed."

"Thank you," said Heck, his face crumbling like gingerbread. "I'm glad to see all is well." He turned slowly on his crutches and made his way out of the room.

Wren sighed. "I don't have time for this," she said, looking over at Dimia. She pointed at Matthias. "Let me know when he can be brought out of the slumber," she said and signed.

Elanor watched her go.

How could Heck ask Ioan to leave? How could he ask any of them to? Josetta was not someone you could run from.

A throat cleared, bringing her out of her thoughts. Two familiar figures were standing in the doorway.

"Bad time?" asked Thackery.

*C*hapter .8

Thackery and Aislynn stepped into the infirmary, snow melting on their shoulders. The princess wore a blue dress and cloak, the hem muddy and torn, her dark hair in a tangle down her back. There was a bag tied at her waist.

Elanor was surprised to see her. Even though she had offered the princess a place in the Mountain after they had been ambushed in the forest, she never imagined Aislynn would take her up on it.

Thackery crossed the room and spun Dimia around. Her face lit up as she pulled him into a tight embrace. Just as Tasmin had raised Elanor and Ioan, the healer had cared for Thackery after he had been rescued from Josetta's palace. They were family.

Dimia set about checking him for injuries until Thackery stopped her.

I'm fine, he signed, then gestured toward the princess. *We're fine.*

Hello, Aislynn signed hesitantly, stepping forward. *It's good to meet you.*

Dimia immediately welcomed her, putting a hand on each of their cheeks, relief evident on her face.

I'm glad you're back, she signed, releasing them.

"Were you successful?" Elanor asked.

Across the room one of the injured Orphans moaned and turned over on her straw mattress.

"Perhaps this is a conversation for somewhere more private," Rhys suggested.

Dimia agreed, ushering them out of the infirmary. Rhys took a moment to embrace both Thackery and Aislynn, and Elanor was relieved when neither seemed to expect the same from her.

"Well?" she asked.

Aislynn pulled a mirror from the bag at her waist and passed it to Elanor. It was small and square, with jewels dotting the handle. One large stone pulsed gently, bright blue, and then quickly faded to white.

"Is it supposed to do that?" Rhys asked.

"I don't know what it's supposed to do," said Aislynn.

"That's the first time I've seen a change since Adviser Hull tried to take it."

"Adviser Hull?" Rhys asked. "I thought Linnea was the one who had it."

"She did." There were dark circles under Aislynn's eyes. "But as soon as she gave it back to me, as we planned, I was threatened by her toad of a husband, Westerly . . . and then by Adviser Hull." She looked exhausted, but there was a fierceness to her gaze. "He was the one who attacked me in the forest, wearing Linnea's ring." Aislynn put her fingers against her throat. There were bruises there, though they had almost faded. "He wanted that." She looked at the mirror, still in Elanor's hands. "He did something with it. He made it glow—white, bright white—and then he was able to force me to move toward him."

"What do you mean he forced you?" Elanor asked, no longer wanting to hold the mirror, which was cold against her palm.

"With magic."

There was a moment of silence.

"That's impossible," said Elanor. "Men can't use magic."

"I can't explain it," Aislynn said, her frustration evident. "But that's what happened. Somehow Hull was using the headmistress's powers. I think it was because of the ring he wore. And I think the mirror is the same. I think it can steal magic."

Chapter .9

It was late, but the lights in the kitchen were blazing brightly, and delicious scents were wafting out into the dining hall, followed by soft humming. The snow falling outside had guaranteed that Tasmin would be cooking tonight. There was nothing the cook enjoyed more than a change in season, and right now half the Mountain smelled of oranges and cloves. And hot, spicy cider.

The others entered the kitchen eagerly, but Elanor hesitated. She was reluctant to see her adoptive mother, especially after their last conversation. She was still angry that Tasmin thought there was anything in this kingdom or beyond that would inspire Elanor to leave the Mountain. But she also knew that avoiding Tasmin and, by extension, the kitchen, was impossible.

Like Aislynn, Tasmin was a royal by birth. But she considered herself a commoner, and no one knew exactly how or when she had come to live in the Mountain. When she spoke about her past, the details were vague and sometimes contradictory. No one seemed to know where she was from or who her family was, though Ioan swore that she had once mentioned having brothers. But she knew things—things about royal life, things that nobody else knew—and she might know something about the mirror or the girls who had been disappearing.

There were four mugs waiting for them, steam hovering above the rims like clouds. Dagger was perched near the stove, peering out between jars of spices. No wonder the fox had gotten so plump.

Dagger darted down the wall, using the uneven stone as footholds to reach the ground, before climbing up Elanor's leg to her shoulder. Even though she was far too big to be sitting there, the fox draped herself across the back of Elanor's neck and licked her chin.

"You've been feeding her too much," said Elanor, taking a thick slice of bread. It had been hours since she had last eaten.

"I have to feed someone while you're gone." Tasmin looked back over her shoulder and smiled at Elanor. It was as close to an apology as either of them would get.

Introductions were made before the mirror was brought out. "We have something to show you," Elanor said, handing it to Tasmin.

This time the stone in the handle glowed bright blue, and everyone leaned closer to look at it.

"Remarkable," said Tasmin.

"I don't understand it," said Aislynn, looking up at her. "There must be a reason for the stone to change the way it does."

"I've never seen anything like this," Tasmin said, passing the mirror back to Elanor. The glow faded, just as it had done before.

There was no hiding the disappointment on Aislynn's face.

"I know it has something to do with the girls who have been disappearing," she said. "And I know Hull's responsible."

"There have always been girls who disappear," said Tasmin, folding her hands. "Girls who fell in love with those they shouldn't have loved, girls who were with child when it wasn't time, or just girls who didn't want to be." She frowned. "There have always been lies to cover up these familial inconveniences."

Aislynn shook her head. "This is different. These girls are

being taken." Her fingers were wrapped around her mug, her jaw set stubbornly. Suddenly the cider began to bubble and hiss. Everyone leaped away from the table, but no one more quickly than Aislynn, whose hands flew to her face.

The cider stopped boiling.

"I'm sorry." Aislynn's cheeks were red, eyes wide. "I thought I was getting better at controlling it."

Thackery wrapped a comforting arm around the princess's shoulders.

Tasmin peered into the mug, now half full. Glancing up at Aislynn, she smiled. "You don't need to control it," she said. "You need to learn how to harness it. And I can help."

As the conversation shifted to training and tutoring, a wave of exhaustion washed over Elanor. The past few days were taking their toll on her, the warmth of the kitchen lulling her into a haze. Then, through the comforting scent of apples and spice, came the sharp, tangy smell of lemon, and Elanor's stomach rolled. Even the slightest hint of lemon overwhelmed her senses, pushing aside anything else. It took her right back to the palace, right back into Josetta's clutches.

She remembered so clearly that first morning as the Queen's servant. Once the tears had been scrubbed from her face, the rest of her body bathed and perfumed, Elanor had been helped into a gray uniform. The fabric was itchy and stiff, deeply uncomfortable for a child who had only worn loose, thin fabrics softened by time. These new clothes were starched and snug, buttoned all the way up to her chin and tight around her wrists.

Once dressed, she had been taken to Josetta's chamber. It was an opulent room, with velvet wallpaper and thick, plush carpeting. To Elanor it felt like the inside of a beating heart, everything bloodred and lush to the touch.

The Queen was seated on one of the large, overstuffed sofas, which was also draped in red. Her gown glittered with thousands of crystals that had been sewn into the satin folds, and there was a smaller version of her fox coat across her shoulders. Each of her fingers was adorned with enormous jewels almost as large as the pearl that hung from her tiara. The tiara itself was an intricate tangle of gold vines and tiny, sharp thorns. It rested on her luminous mane of red hair, which surrounded her face like spun fire.

"Dried those tears, I see," said Josetta. She was making notations in a large tome that had a harp, the Queen's symbol, embossed on the front.

Elanor managed a nod.

"Yes, Your Majesty," Josetta prompted, not looking up from her writing.

"Yes, Your Majesty," Elanor repeated obediently.

"I will not remind you of your manners again."

There was a knock at the door. "Come in," the Queen said.

A man entered. He was tall and well dressed. Not handsome, but he carried himself with the confidence of someone who thought himself so. His hair was dark, with a smudge of gray at each temple, and his skin was pale. But unlike the Queen's porcelain complexion, his was pallid and slightly green, as if he was ill. Thin, dark eyebrows sat close to his eyes, and his high forehead, combined with a downturned mouth, made it appear as though he was scowling.

"Cyril." Josetta rose to greet him. He kissed her hands lingeringly, pressing his cheek against them. The Queen seemed to stiffen at his touch, but the smile remained fixed on her face. "So glad you could come."

"You know I am your humble servant," he said, clearly reluctant to release her from his grip. "You need only summon me."

"Yes," said Josetta, pulling her hands away and lifting her head high. She was nearly as tall as he was, and he was very tall. "You are quite . . . accommodating." Her tone indicated that it was not something to be proud of.

"Is your husband not joining us?" Cyril asked, though he

sat before she answered. He chose the settee that she had been sitting on.

Josetta pressed her lips together and perched on a different sofa. Frowning at the cushions, she rearranged them until they pleased her. "You know he never takes an interest in such matters."

Cyril seemed to notice Elanor for the first time. "Will we have company for our entire visit?" His eyes were pale gray and flat, like something dead. Elanor shuddered.

"Lunch will be here soon. Are you feeling adventurous today?"

Cyril sneered. "No, of course not."

"She'll leave once we're done."

There was another knock, and several servants entered with silver trays heavy with food. A table at one end of the room was set, and once the servants departed, Cyril ushered Josetta to her chair before taking a seat of his own. He placed his napkin across his lap and waited. For a moment no one moved, and Elanor was afraid that someone had cast a spell, freezing them in place. She wiggled her pinkie finger to make sure she hadn't been affected. Then Josetta turned to look at her expectantly.

"Well, go on," she said, gesturing to her plate. "Try it."

Elanor felt her skin prickle at the intensity of the Queen's gaze. She bowed her head, trying to avoid her sharp green eyes. "I couldn't, Your Majesty."

"Don't be pumpkin headed," Josetta said impatiently, shoving the plate in Elanor's direction. "It's what you're here for. Try the food."

The plate was piled high with red meat and potatoes and onions and greens. With her hand shaking, Elanor took a tiny forkful of the main course. It smelled amazing and tasted wonderful—the liver of a boar, perfectly salted. She quickly set the fork down and stepped back from the table. "Ah-ah-ah," Josetta said. "You need to try everything, my pet, including the dessert."

So Elanor tried it all. The caramelized onions that nearly melted in her mouth, the gravy-dipped potatoes, and the crisp, bright greens. And the dessert. A lemon tart, with a crust that burst into buttery crumbs on her tongue and a bittersweet lemon custard that slid down her throat and made her cough.

She could feel Josetta's eyes on her with each bite she took. Finally she bowed and stepped back from the table. But Josetta stopped her again.

"Now Cyril's plate," she said.

His food tasted just as good. But this time the tartness of the lemon burned her tongue. She didn't like it. And she certainly didn't like the way that the Queen and Cyril were looking at her, as if they were expecting something to happen.

After a few moments, Cyril picked up his fork.

"She's still alive," he said. "Let's eat."

That was Elanor's childhood. She was summoned throughout the day, every day, to taste Josetta's meals. And no matter what was served, there was always a lemon tart to accompany it. It was rumored that there was a lemon tree in one of the rooms of the massive castle, grown there for the sole purpose of making the Queen's tarts. It was tended by a servant whose only role was to keep the tree bearing fruit.

Chapter .10

The Mountain was quiet and still by the time they headed to bed, all of them disappointed. There were no answers to their questions about the mirror and no place to start searching for them.

When Elanor woke the next morning, Dagger was gone, having left a trail of coarse hair across the pillow and blankets. It was rare for the little fox to rise before Elanor, but by the stiffness of her limbs, she could tell she had slept for a long time. The rumble in her stomach confirmed it, so Elanor dressed and went in search of food and her friend.

She knew full well where Dagger tended to spend her days, and sure enough, Elanor found her in the infirmary, making her rounds. When Elanor entered, Dagger was curled gently around Matthias's head, almost like an orange-and-black pillow.

The little fox seemed to gravitate toward the injured. Elanor traced the scar on her neck, remembering how confused she had been when Dagger kept lying across her throat after she had been woken from the slumber.

"She's trying to heal you," Tasmin had said. "It's the only way she knows how."

And that's what the fox was doing now, with Matthias. The peaceful expression on his face seemed to indicate that it was helping.

The room was quiet—Dimia's needles and knitting were in her chair, but the healer was nowhere to be seen. Ioan, too, was gone, as was one of the other injured Orphans. Only two of the beds were currently occupied. Elanor took a seat next to Dagger's patient, observing how the fox's breathing matched his.

Since last night Matthias had been made a little more comfortable. His shoes had been removed, his clothes appeared to be freshly washed, and he was covered with a thick quilt. The bruises on his face were gone, as was the cut on his lip, and the bandage around his head had been discarded. His hair was clean, but still a little wet, making the curls more pronounced. Elanor had never seen anyone with his features, the dark skin and red hair, but she found it to be a pleasing combination. Handsome. She especially liked the way his ears stuck out.

She hadn't been sitting there long when Heck came in, leaning heavily on his crutches. Usually he wore a wooden prosthetic to compensate for the missing lower half of his left leg, but Elanor knew the winter was hard on him and other Orphans with similar injuries.

"Dimia's not here," she said, rising to her feet. The last thing she wanted was for Heck to try to convince her to leave the Mountain. If she was honest with herself, she would know that she wasn't being fair. Not to him or anyone who wanted to go with him. No one should have to live the life they had lived.

Heck seemed to sense her discomfort. He gave her a small smile as he settled onto one of the cots.

"Dimia said she had a poultice that would make me feel like a royal at her first ball."

"I'm sure she'll be back soon," said Elanor. "I should . . ." She gestured toward the door.

"Wren was looking for you," he said, ignoring her attempt to leave. "Apparently Josetta has been eyeing a small village toward the north. There's been word that some of the villagers are less than eager to pledge allegiance to the Wicked Queen."

"And yet most will," Elanor said. After all these years, after everything they knew about Josetta and what she did to her followers, Elanor should be shocked that there were still commoners who willingly joined her. But she wasn't.

"Fear can make people do terrible things," said Heck.

"I have no doubt," Elanor said, more sharply than she intended. She had no right to act superior.

"I'm not ashamed of leaving." His words were quiet. "I'm not ashamed to say that I don't want to fight anymore."

"Not all of us have that choice."

"You always have a choice." Heck's gaze was steady.

But he didn't understand. He didn't know that Elanor had a debt to pay. One that might never be forgiven.

All willing Orphans were gathered together in the dining cavern. Wren had command of the room and waved Elanor to the front when she entered.

"There are at least four families who want to leave," she was saying. "The huntsmen are set to depart from the palace in the next few days, and we plan to be gone before they arrive."

Wren was the only Orphan who patrolled by herself, disappearing for days on end and returning with no explanation of where she had been. But she often came back with valuable information on the huntsmen, information that had saved lives on more than one occasion. No one asked where the information came from, and Wren had made it clear that after what she had been through at Josetta's hands, she didn't owe anyone an answer.

"We'll need at least a dozen, more if they can be spared." Wren glanced over at Bronwyn, who nodded. This was not going to be a small rescue, like the ones Brigid and Thackery had helped with during their time at Elderwood. No lone little girl needing to be relocated. These were families who needed new homes. New lives.

Elanor took a seat next to Rhys and Ioan, both of whom looked eager to volunteer. At the other end of the room, Thackery and Aislynn sat stiffly next to each other. Aislynn's jaw was set, and Elanor noticed that her fingers were curved protectively around the bag still tied to her hip.

"The families will be taken to a safe house in the north," Wren continued. "Those who volunteer to take them there should plan to be gone for several weeks, at the least. It's not a short journey from the village."

Elanor assumed Wren was talking about Aislynn's family home, which might explain the tension radiating off both the princess and Thackery. Sure enough, the moment Wren stopped talking, Thackery turned to Aislynn. But before he could say anything, she stood and approached Elanor.

"I was told I should speak to you about weapons," she said. Wisely Rhys and Ioan took that as their cue to scatter.

"You're not ready," Thackery said, coming up behind her.

"I did not ask for your opinion on the matter," the princess said primly before turning back to Elanor. "I need a weapon."

"You're not going on this mission," insisted Thackery.

"Don't think for a moment that you can control me," said Aislynn, turning on him. "I've spent my whole life being told what to do, and I gave up everything I hold dear so I could make my own decisions."

Thackery's face went bright red.

"I'm sorry," he said. "That's not what I meant to do."

"I just want to help." Aislynn's expression softened. "I want to be useful."

"You're not useful to us dead." Wren had joined the group. "You need to be trained before you can come on missions. You need to learn how to fight."

"I know how to fight," Aislynn insisted. "Remember how well I did in the forest?"

"I remember that you almost passed out because you used magic to kill someone," Elanor interjected. "You were going on instinct. You need more than that to survive."

"So train me," said Aislynn eagerly. "I'm one of you now."

"You're not one of us." Wren crossed her arms over her chest, taking a long look at the former princess. "But maybe you could be."

Chapter .11

They stopped just on the outskirts of the village, nearly a day from the Mountain. Snow had fallen heavily, and the Orphans were knee-deep in it. Elanor had made sure to dress properly, as it wouldn't help to be distracted by chilled hands or ill-fitting shoes. The bloodstain had been scrubbed from her jacket, which was snug over the layers of cotton and wool. Her neck was wrapped with one of Dimia's knit scarves, her toes warm in socks made by the healer as well. But still, when the wind blew, Elanor felt it all the way to her bones. She clenched her teeth to keep them from chattering and waited with the others for the first scout to return.

The news, when it arrived, was encouraging. Though the

rebellious families had been locked away in one of the houses, they were being guarded by other commoners who had few weapons and likely very little training. There had been no sign of huntsmen.

But the Orphans had been fooled before. So Elanor and the others now waited for the second scout to return, the one who had made a wider circle around the village, looking for signs of an intended ambush.

Rubbing her hands together, Elanor scanned the landscape, searching for hidden huntsmen as well as locations they might be able to use if they needed to fall back during a fight. It looked as though the forest had recently survived a fire. The trunks of the barren trees were blackened and crumbling, but still standing. The snowy ground was uneven, all frozen ditches and icy hills, both capable of providing cover. If necessary, there would be places to hide.

"Did you speak to Ioan before we left?" Rhys joined her, his voice barely audible above the wind.

"No," Elanor said, keeping her own voice low. "I imagine he wasn't pleased that he had to stay in the Mountain."

"I'm not so sure about that," Rhys said. "I saw him talking to Heck the other night. Making plans, I think."

So Ioan was thinking of leaving. The ache of betrayal rose in Elanor's chest, but there was nothing she could do. If Ioan wanted to leave the Mountain, that was his choice.

He had asked her once what she would do if they killed the Queen. He asked her what she would want to do. And she had wondered. Wondered what her life would be like if she could be a girl instead of a soldier. What would she see then, looking out over this landscape? Would she still see places to hide, ways to protect herself? Or would she see something new? Something beautiful? Something that had no purpose beyond just existing?

But Elanor couldn't imagine that life. Because even if there was a world beyond this, even if there was a way to live without fighting, without fear, she could not picture herself in it.

She planned to die for this cause. Maybe that would bring forgiveness.

There was a flurry of activity. The second scout had returned. Elanor followed Rhys, taking high, careful steps through the snow, to where everyone had gathered. A circle formed around Wren.

"There have been no signs of huntsmen, but that doesn't mean they're not there. We'll divide into three groups. Those who will be accompanying the villagers to the north will wait in the forest. Half the others will provide the distraction for the guards; the other half will lead the families into the woods.

Everyone should be armed and alert, no matter their position."

It was an unnecessary order, as everyone had already drawn their weapons. Thackery had a firm grip on his sword, his mouth flattened into a tense line. His expression was mimicked by the others. Elanor felt a jolt of anticipation. This was the world she knew. This was the life she chose.

As soon as they set foot in the village, Elanor knew that something was wrong. It appeared to be deserted—there was no one around the two dozen or so cottages that circled the town square except for two men, commoners by their dress. Both were armed with staffs and knives. But they were too calm, too relaxed. Elanor tensed as Wren approached the guards, a hand on her undrawn sword.

"Best step aside," Wren said.

They did not, exchanging a look instead. The door of the cottage behind them was locked with an enormous padlock, and from inside came the sound of people pounding against the wood, their words muffled. Elanor's mouth was dry. Her eyes darted around looking for the huntsmen who were surely there. Waiting.

Wren drew her sword. "No need to make this bloody."

One of the men smiled. "You'll regret that, pretty," he said, reaching toward her.

She moved away easily. But Elanor sucked in a breath when she saw the man's forearm. There was a harp burned into his wrist. Josetta's mark.

"They're huntsmen!" Elanor yelled, though Wren already had her blade against his throat. Before the other could reach for his knife, an arrow came flying out of the forest, striking him between the eyes. With a gurgle, he fell to the ground.

All around them, the doors to the other cottages smashed open as huntsmen poured into the town square, yelling and clanking, their armor creating a dense wall of sound. A battle cry bursting from her throat, Elanor charged into the crowd, using her small stature to avoid swinging swords and axes. The heavy breast and arm plates might protect the huntsmen from the arrows flying out of the forest, but they also made them slow and awkward.

Elanor took a running leap and catapulted herself onto the back of a huntsman. Clinging to his shoulders with one arm, she drove her ax into the exposed part of his neck. Blood gushed from the wound as he toppled forward. She used the momentum of his falling body to crash into another soldier, the impact knocking him to the ground. A swing of her ax made quick work of him. After all, they were much easier to dispatch when they were on their knees.

Her fingers were sticky with blood as she threw herself

back into the melee. Thackery, easy to spot because of his height, was locked in an uneven duel. The huntsman was twice his width, his sword swinging dangerously close to Thackery's exposed neck. Elanor sprinted toward them. With a shout, she leaped at the huntsman's knees, using her entire weight to knock him back and over her shoulder. He hit the ground hard, his sword skidding away. There was no need for Elanor to stop. She knew Thackery would be able to finish him off.

It was impossible to know who was winning. All around were screams of pain and cries of victory. The air whistled with arrows shot from the Orphans hiding in the trees.

She passed Wren, whose face was bloody but grinning as she dispatched a huntsman with a rock, and Elanor heard the sickening crack of bone against stone. Keeping her fingers wrapped around the handle of her ax, Elanor swallowed the sour bile of battle and headed toward the prisoners' cottage, which was still locked.

Two swings of the blade were all it took—Elanor knew the importance of a freshly sharpened weapon—and the door burst open, prisoners streaming out, wide-eyed and terrified. With a whistle, Elanor alerted those waiting in the forest. But before she could catch sight of Rhys, a huntsman's fist slammed into her jaw.

Elanor saw stars, but they didn't stop her from striking

back, her ax swinging forward and blindly finding its target. When her vision cleared, Elanor saw that the fallen huntsman was a young girl, only a few years old than she was. For a moment Elanor was frozen. It had been a long time since she had seen a soldier so young. Like Elanor, the girl's hair was black, her helmet discarded in the mud next to her.

"Watch out!" someone shouted, and Elanor whirled around.

A charging huntsman stopped in his tracks, his mouth filling with blood as a broadhead pierced his throat. He collapsed in front of Elanor, but before she could leap over his body, a hand fisted itself in the back of her jacket and yanked her off her feet. She was thrown to the ground.

The earth was hot and wet beneath her palms. A hammer, like the one she used on her anvil, thudded into the dirt next to her, just barely missing her hand. Her ax escaped her grasp. Elanor rolled out of the way as the heavy hammer came down again, this time brushing her hip.

The huntsman with the hammer spat into the dirt. He was enormous, taller than Wren, wider than Ioan, and stronger than all of them. Despite the cold, his arms were bare and swollen with thick veins and muscle. As Elanor scrambled to her hands and knees, his foot swung out, landing squarely in her gut. She dropped to the ground, her face slamming into the blood and muck that now ran in rivulets through the town.

Still her fingers found the knife at her hip, and when he raised his hammer again, she could see clearly the tender spot where his chest plate pulled away, leaving the great veins in his neck exposed. Elanor released her knife just as he slammed down the hammer. It drove into her leg, tearing flesh and breaking bone. Pain blackened her sight, but before it went dark, she saw that her knife had found a place in the huntsman's neck, and his blood joined the river that flowed around them.

Chapter .12

When Elanor woke, she was in motion and she couldn't feel her leg. The front of her body was pressed against something warm and damp. Stickiness coated her eyelids, and she made several attempts to open them before she managed it.

She was tied to someone's back, her arms draped limply over shoulders, her legs held in place by whoever was carrying her. Something was also wrapped around her waist. She blinked several times to clear the blurriness from her vision. The back of Thackery's head came into view.

Still she could not feel one of her legs.

"Stop," she said, her voice sounding miles away. "Stop," she said again, more clearly.

Thackery slowed, but only for a moment. He briefly glanced back at her before resuming his steady march through the trees.

"How do you feel?" he asked, his voice low, beads of sweat on his forehead despite the cold.

Humiliated, Elanor thought, the events leading to her current situation returning to her. The ambush in the village, the surge of huntsmen, the hammer crushing her leg. The leg that was numb.

Elanor soon realized that they were not alone in the forest. Half a dozen Orphans surrounded them, some carrying others on their back, some with weapons drawn.

"Where are the others?" Elanor asked, her mouth dry. "Where's Rhys?" He had been in the forest during the attack.

"He's safe," Thackery said. "Wren and Rhys are leading the rescued villagers to the Northern Kingdom. How's your leg?"

"I can't feel it," she said. She couldn't see it, either. Just holding up her head took enormous effort. Trying to examine parts of her body seemed like a fool's errand.

"It's broken," Thackery said. "Pretty badly, too. One of the healers did the best she could, wrapped and numbed it, but you need Dimia."

Elanor nodded. She knew what could happen if injuries like this one went untreated.

"How far are we from the Mountain?"

"Not far," Thackery said. "Nightfall if we're lucky."

She looked around. It was hard to tell at first what time of day it was, with the gray gloom of winter coloring the sky. But behind the clouds was the faintest hint of the sun, just beginning its descent. Midday.

Elanor tried not to think about the pain that was creeping back into her leg or the awkwardness of being carried by Thackery and focused, instead, on the forest. Who knew what might be nearby?

But the day passed and the forest remained silent, except for hushed conversations and hurried footsteps. It used to be that the Orphans couldn't go a stone's throw beyond the barrier without discovering a patrol of huntsmen. Now Elanor had trouble remembering the last time she had seen one of Josetta's soldiers within a mile of the Mountain.

Had the Queen abandoned her search for the Orphan's camp in favor of expanding her kingdom? And why did that possibility, instead of giving Elanor comfort, only send a jolt of fear through her?

The wounded were laid onto cots in the infirmary, and Dimia fluttered around them, examining injuries and prioritizing healing. Elanor got a glimpse of her leg and wished she hadn't.

It was swollen and twisted, like an overcooked carrot. The numbing spell the healer had given her at the village had worn off hours ago, but Elanor had not wanted to stop the group to have it recast, so she'd bitten a hole in her cheek instead. The entire limb throbbed like a terrible toothache.

Elanor lay back on the straw mattress and closed her eyes, trying to ignore the moans and mutterings all around her. She had sensed that something was wrong when they entered the village but had said nothing. Was the blood of those who had fallen, those they had left behind, on her hands? Yes. But not just because of today. If she had been braver all those years ago, things would have been different. Everything would have been different.

Guilt, bitter and familiar, spread across her tongue.

A gentle hand on her swollen, painful knee made Elanor's eyes fly open. Her teeth found the inside of her cheek, and a fresh gush of blood filled her mouth.

Dimia smiled down at her. "You'll be fine," she said slowly. *With lots of rest.*

With a nod, Elanor turned her head to the side, embarrassed by the hot itch of tears in the corners of her eyes. She refused to let them fall. On the cot next to her was Matthias, still under the influence of the slumber. Wrapped around his head was Dagger, also sleeping deeply.

As Dimia placed her warm hands on Elanor's leg and the hum of magic surrounded them, Elanor reached out and ran a gentle finger down Dagger's soft forehead. The little fox opened her eyes, blinked, and then yawned.

By the time Dimia had rewrapped Elanor's leg and ordered her on strict bed rest for the next few days, Dagger had found her way to Elanor's cot and was stretched out along the length of her injured limb. With the fox snoring beside her, Elanor closed her eyes again and slept.

Tasmin was the first to visit, and came, as she usually did, bearing food. This time it was fresh bread sweetened with cinnamon and sugar. The dough melted in Elanor's mouth and was warm and sticky on her fingers.

"A recipe from Aislynn," said Tasmin, lifting Dagger off the cot. The fox squirmed at first but soon settled into the cook's wide lap. "Dimia says she hasn't left your side."

"She thinks she's being useful," Elanor said, her mouth full.

"Isn't she?" asked Tasmin with raised eyebrows. "You seem to be healing nicely."

Though it was well bandaged, Elanor could already see that most of the swelling was gone, and her leg was as straight as it had been before. Already she was eager to get out of bed, to get out of the infirmary. But she resisted the urge and settled for wiggling her toes instead. They waved pleasantly at her from the end of the bed.

"He's been here for a while." Tasmin was looking at the next cot, where Matthias was still under the influence of the slumber.

"He hit his head pretty hard," said Elanor. Someone had removed his shirt, presumably to change it or clean it, just as they had done for Elanor. A blanket was drawn up beneath his arms, but most of his chest and his shoulders were still exposed. Elanor had never seen such smooth, unblemished skin before. There was not a single scar visible. Apparently there were still people this world left unwounded.

"Thackery said the mission was successful," Tasmin said.

"I suppose." Elanor leaned back against her pillow. She thought of the village, now deserted, its people gone, its streets covered in blood. And all those who had left willingly. "How can people still join her?" she asked. "How did she gain so much power?"

Tasmin sighed. "Josetta may be wicked, but she's clever, too. She saw how the other royals treated us, and she used it to gain loyalty, to turn us against those who ruled us. Once we did, there was nowhere else to go. We had betrayed those who might have protected us, who could have helped us."

Elanor had heard of the Western Kingdom's monarch king. He had surrendered his palace to Josetta in one of her first victories as the self-proclaimed ruler of the Midlands. From what Elanor knew of her history, it had not taken much to convince the subjects of a vindictive king to betray their master. He had been a cruel and vicious man who treated his servants like slaves. But he had never branded them.

"Josetta gave you a worse life than the one you left."

Tasmin shook her head. "It's easy to look at what she's done now and believe that you would have seen what was coming. We thought she would help us. We trusted her. And there is no shame in trust."

"Tell that to the families now trapped behind her castle walls," Elanor muttered.

But Tasmin ignored her. "Ioan wanted me to talk to you." She scratched Dagger behind her ears.

Elanor looked away from Matthias and back up at her mother. "He's unable to speak to me himself?" But she already knew what Tasmin was going to say.

"He's decided to leave with Heck and the others."

"I see."

Expecting it didn't mean that it felt any less like a betrayal. Elanor clicked her tongue to get Dagger's attention. The little fox immediately uncurled from Tasmin's lap and made the graceful leap into Elanor's arms. Elanor held her against her chest and took a deep sniff of the fox's fur. She smelled like the Mountain, like smoke and home.

"And you?" Elanor finally asked, afraid of the answer. "Will you be leaving as well?"

Tasmin took Elanor's hand. "Do you remember what I told you at the beginning?"

When Elanor had been brought to the Mountain, she had been very sick. Her throat had been ruined, and she had been unable to speak or eat. Tasmin, who knew about plants and poisons and all sorts of strange things, had known what to give Elanor to make her better. But she hadn't known how to heal her. How to reach her.

Even after Elanor began to recover, she had refused the food that was brought to her. She knew it wouldn't be long before the Orphans discovered the truth. That she didn't deserve to be rescued. That she didn't deserve to live. They would find out what she had done, and they would get rid of her.

One morning when Tasmin came to visit Elanor, she'd brought a gift.

"Be careful," she had said, handing over a blanket. Wrapped inside, curled up tight, was a tiny kit, its entire torso thick with bandages. "She got caught in a trap, but whoever set it didn't want her, so they left her to die. We need someone to watch over her while she heals."

Elanor had looked at the kit's tail, knowing exactly why she had been discarded. Besides being too young, her fur was not completely red. Instead it was mottled with black, and the Queen had no use for imperfect pelts.

"I'm no good with healing," Elanor had said.

"She doesn't need to be healed. She needs to be cared for."

"I can't."

"I'm sorry to hear that," Tasmin had said, reaching out for the fox.

But Elanor hadn't let go. "What will happen to it?"

"We'll have to release her and hope the Four Sisters watch out for her." Tasmin had looked down at the bundle in Elanor's arms. "Or pray that they take her without bringing her any more pain."

A part of Elanor had known that she was bluffing. She had considered handing the fox back to Tasmin, showing her that she couldn't be tricked. But then Dagger let out the tiniest of sighs, and Elanor didn't want to let go, not even to prove a point.

"What does she eat?" Elanor had asked.

Tasmin had brought her a bowl of mush. Without hesitating, Elanor took a spoonful and tasted it. It was the first bit of food she had had since that night. Her throat was still sore and it hurt to swallow, but it was good.

"I can get you another bowl for yourself," Tasmin had said.

"I'm not eating it," Elanor had said. "I'm tasting it."

It took almost a season for Elanor to eat food just for herself. And Tasmin never once asked why. She never questioned why one morning Elanor asked for an entire lemon. And she said nothing when Elanor ate that lemon, rind, seeds, and all. Said nothing when Elanor's stomach rejected the sour fruit and burned a new path in Elanor's throat as the lemon returned to the table in a pulpy, foamy mess. But once it had been cleaned away and Elanor's face had been washed and a warm blanket wrapped around her and her fox, Tasmin had taken Elanor's hands.

"You are my family now," she had said. "And I will never let anyone hurt you."

Chapter .13

On the morning of Elanor's fifth day in the infirmary, Dimia decided it was time to bring Matthias out of the slumber. It was also the first time Elanor was allowed out of bed, though she was not permitted to go far or walk without crutches. So she paced the room, stretching her legs, while Dimia prepared the spell.

Elanor was careful to keep her recovering leg extended as she hobbled from one end of the infirmary to the other. After only a few laps, she found herself frustratingly exhausted and collapsed back onto her cot. Dagger, who had been watching her progress from the bed, immediately jumped onto her lap.

Is he going to be all right? Elanor asked Dimia, who was leaning over Matthias.

We won't know until we wake him, she responded before placing her hand over his eyes. A pulse of magic surrounded his body. Elanor could feel the edges of it lapping at her like a river before it retreated completely.

Suddenly Matthias let out a loud gasp, his eyes opening wide.

How are you feeling? Dimia signed, leaning over him.

He stared at her for a moment, his eyebrows furrowing in confusion.

"She asked how you're feeling," Elanor said. His gaze swung to her. There was surprise, but also a flash of recognition.

"Elanor," he murmured, closing his eyes again.

Dimia looked over at Elanor, who shrugged and poked at his foot. His eyes flew open.

"How are you feeling?" Elanor asked again.

"Oh." Matthias pushed himself to a sitting position. "Better, I think," he said, his voice hoarse. He looked at Dimia, who was looking over at Elanor as she translated his statement. "How do I . . ." He gestured vaguely with his hands.

Elanor showed him how to say that he was feeling better.

Drink this. Dimia gave him a mug, with steam curling from it.

"What is it?" he asked.

"Dimia calls it 'the kiss,'" said Elanor. "It will help wake you up."

He took a careful sip and another and then swallowed the rest in one go.

"Thank you," he said, looking at Elanor, who showed him the proper sign. *Thank you*, he repeated.

As Dimia examined Matthias's head, Elanor examined the rest of him. He was handsome, even more so now that he didn't look like he was on the verge of dying. There was a flush to his cheeks, which were indented with more dimples than she had noticed before. His hair was thick and curly. It rested cloudlike on his forehead, and the reddish hue reminded Elanor of summer thunderstorms. But mostly she liked his ears.

The examination complete, Dimia turned away from their little group and began tending to her other patients. It wasn't until Matthias glanced over at Elanor that she realized she'd been staring, and it wasn't until their eyes met that she noticed her palms were damp. She looked away. She didn't have time for this.

But Dagger seemed to have none of the same qualms. Before Elanor could stop her, the little fox had made the dainty leap from her lap to Matthias's chest. He grunted a little in surprise.

"Hello," he said to the fox, who peered curiously at him.

"Dagger likes to be in the way," said Elanor, reaching out to remove her pet.

But Matthias shook his head, stopping her. "I don't mind," he said. "She won't bite me, will she?"

"Not unless you get between her and her food."

He smiled, and the dimples deepened. "I wouldn't dream of it." Slowly he lifted a hand, which Dagger sniffed. And then licked. "I think she likes me," Matthias said, scratching behind the fox's ears.

"She spent a lot of time with you when you were in the slumber," Elanor told him.

"I remember," he said, to Elanor's surprise.

"Most people find the slumber somewhat unpleasant," she said.

"Some of it was." Matthias was now getting his chin rubbed by Dagger's nose. "But sometimes I would feel this presence, this warmth, right here." He raised a hand to the side of his head where his injury had been, where Dagger had slept. "And the bad dreams would go away."

"I'm glad she could give you some relief," said Elanor.

Only a few years after Elanor had been brought to the Mountain—after she had been given Dagger and nursed her back to health, after Elanor had pledged her loyalty to the

Orphans—she had been injured in a mission like the one that had just broken her leg. But that injury had been far more severe. She hadn't been the soldier she was now and had gotten her neck slashed by a huntsman's knife. If it hadn't been for Rhys, she might have died right there in that village.

He had wrapped most of his shirt around her throat and found the healer that had come on the mission with them. Once she had closed the wound and put Elanor into the slumber, Rhys had carried Elanor all the way back to the Mountain.

When they had arrived in the infirmary, Dagger was waiting. The entire time Elanor was in the slumber, the little fox had not left her side. Elanor ran her fingers over that raised line, now remembering how foolish she had been to leave her back unguarded. It was a mistake she had not made since.

"How long have I been here?" asked Matthias, still pampering the fox now curled up on his chest. Some of the peacefulness had left his face, and a crease had formed between his eyebrows.

"A few weeks," said Elanor, watching the frown deepen.

"My friends," he said quietly.

"The Elders will want to speak to you again," said Elanor. "Now that you're awake."

But Matthias was looking past her, toward the doorway.

Elanor turned. Her brother stood there, twisting his hands nervously.

"You're awake," he said to Matthias.

"Only just," Matthias replied.

"Your head?"

"Better."

Ioan smiled, but he avoided Elanor's gaze.

Matthias cleared his throat and closed his eyes. Across the room, Dimia was also doing her best to give Elanor and Ioan some semblance of privacy, though it hardly seemed necessary.

"I already know," Elanor said. "Tasmin told me."

"I should have told you." Ioan took a seat next to her on the cot. "Can you forgive me?"

"For what?" she asked. "For not telling me or for leaving?"

"For both."

Elanor had learned long ago that it was impossible to stay mad at Ioan. It was the way he always looked so innocent. How could anyone blame a face like that? Not to mention how sorry he always was, how apologetic. Elanor had stopped counting the number of times she had started a conversation angry with him and ended up being the one apologizing.

But she wasn't jealous of him anymore. Yes, he was charming and charismatic, but she was strong and fast. And considering how often Ioan found himself in trouble, she knew she was better off with her talents instead of his. You couldn't charm an arrow when it was headed right toward your heart.

Perhaps it was better that he left the Mountain. He would be safer; that much would be certain. He wouldn't volunteer for dangerous missions or take unnecessary risks. Elanor wouldn't have to worry about him so much.

"Of course I can forgive you," Elanor said, and wondered why it was so easy to forgive him and so difficult to forgive herself.

*C*hapter .14

Carved into the wall of the dining cavern was a map of the Midlands. It had been there when Elanor first arrived at the Mountain, but it changed often. Years ago it had been a fraction of what it was now, showing the area between the Orphans' hiding place and the Queen's palace. Now mirroring the expansion of Josetta's rule, the map dominated the great wall.

Leaning heavily on her crutch, Elanor placed her hand against the etchings that represented her home. The rock was cold beneath her palm as she traced the world beyond the barrier. There were small notches in the map, made to note how many huntsmen had been discovered throughout the

Midlands. The notches representing the soldiers who had been killed were painted red, while the notches representing those who had escaped were left untouched. Each grouping had been circled and given a color to indicate the year the attack had occurred.

Elanor scanned the map for this year's attacks, which were marked with a bright grass green. She spotted the most recent skirmish with Josetta's men, the one she had been lucky to survive. Satisfaction filled her when she saw how many of the notches were painted red. Far more than half.

The other bright green skirmishes were all near the border or toward the northern side of the Midland's castle. Elanor looked for last year's attacks, marked in pale lavender. The map revealed the same pattern. It had been almost two years since huntsmen had been encountered near the Mountain. Josetta had stopped looking for them, it seemed. Still, Elanor felt uneasy.

When she returned to the infirmary, Bronwyn was seated on one of the cots, in the middle of a discussion with Matthias. His hands were fisted in his lap. Even from the doorway, Elanor could see that his shoulders were tense and he was not looking at the Elder, but rather at the floor.

"I need to help my friends," he was saying. At the end of his cot was Dagger, meticulously cleaning her paws.

"They might not be alive," said Bronwyn.

If it hadn't been for the pain in Elanor's leg, she might have retreated quietly from the room, leaving the two of them to their discussion. But her trek to the dining cavern had exhausted her, and the infirmary cot looked too tempting to pass up. Her crutch scraped against the floor, and both Bronwyn and Matthias turned toward her as she hobbled across the room. Carefully she swung herself onto the mattress. Immediately Dagger abandoned her grooming and made her way to Elanor's lap.

"I didn't mean to interrupt," Elanor said, giving the fox a pat.

"I had also hoped to speak to you," said Bronwyn, turning away from Matthias, whose jaw was as tight as his shoulders.

His eyes met Elanor's, his frustration obvious, and she felt a twinge of sympathy for him. Bronwyn was right—his friends were quite possibly dead. And if they weren't, it was likely they had been recruited by the Queen. Which fate was worse depended on whom you asked. Matthias quickly dropped his gaze again, his hands twisted into white-knuckled knots.

Bronwyn sat down next to Elanor. "The royal has declared her intent to join us," she said. There was displeasure in both her voice and expression.

"Aislynn?"

"She said that you offered her a place here," said Bronwyn.

"I did." Adjusting her injured leg on the sagging cot, Elanor met the Elder's eye. "We need the help."

"I would hardly consider her offer helpful." Bronwyn's skepticism was clear. "She's unpolished and clumsy."

"Much like I was, I'm sure." Elanor knew that Bronwyn was right to be wary of outsiders. But she also knew that when Heck and Ioan and the others left, those remaining in the Mountain would be in need of help, no matter how clumsy. "I'll train her," she said, scratching a blissful Dagger behind her ears.

"Good." Bronwyn rose. "We will discuss her future once she learns how to throw a dagger without pricking herself."

"As you wish, Elder," Elanor said, dipping her head respectfully.

After Bronwyn left, Elanor sat there, staring at her bruised and bandaged leg. It was already frustrating being stuck in the infirmary, but now that she had something to do, she was especially eager to get back on her feet.

"You—you can teach someone how to fight?" asked Matthias.

Elanor looked up and saw the eager gleam in his eyes.

"Depends on the student," she said, lying down and closing her eyes.

She knew that Aislynn, despite being ill prepared for war, could be transformed into a fighter. After all, no one had been more inexperienced than Elanor when she had chosen her first weapon. Aislynn would learn to fight for the same reason that Elanor had—because she needed to.

Days later Elanor was still depending heavily on her crutch, but felt recovered enough to return to her room. Running her hand over her neatly made bed, complete with Dagger napping on the pillow, she heard Aislynn before she saw her.

"We'll have to work on your stealth," said Elanor, not turning around.

"Among other things, I'm sure," the princess said.

Elanor glanced over her shoulder to find Aislynn lingering in the doorway, her hands clenched at her sides. Unlike everyone else in the Mountain, she was wearing a dress. Though it was a simple and serviceable green garment— not the expensive gown she had arrived in—Aislynn was still inappropriately clothed.

"First off," said Elanor, taking a seat on her bed, "we'll need to get you some pants." To her surprise, Aislynn balked. "Is that a problem?" Elanor asked.

"No," said Aislynn immediately. "No." She looked down at the dress, her lips twisted in a wry smile. "They've been offered. I—I've had a hard time letting go of some things." Uncurling her hands, Aislynn smoothed down the fabric at her waist. "Pants. I'll make sure to wear them next time."

"Good," said Elanor. "Here." She tossed the princess a knife, which Aislynn struggled to catch.

When she finally grabbed hold of it, it was by the blade. Luckily the knife was sheathed. Elanor took a deep breath, preparing herself for the hard work ahead.

"I want you to attack me," she said, leaning her crutch against the bed.

"Attack you?" Aislynn looked up from the knife with shock. "But you're injured."

"Unfortunately I don't think that will give you an advantage," said Elanor. "Besides, I have a weapon, too." She held up her own unsheathed knife.

"I don't want to hurt you," Aislynn argued.

"I don't want that, either. Though, I would be impressed if you did." Placing the knife in her lap, Elanor scooted back on the soft mattress. "Come on," she said. "Attack me."

"I don't think this is a good idea," Aislynn muttered as she pulled her knife from its sheath. "Ouch."

A smear of blood appeared on her fingers, a few drops spilling onto the floor.

Elanor resisted the urge to roll her eyes, trying to remember how uncoordinated she had been the first time she had picked up a dagger.

"Avoid the blade," she said.

Cheeks red, Aislynn nodded and grasped the knife by its handle. She left herself completely exposed, her arm held awkwardly in front of her chest.

"Attack me," Elanor said again.

Aislynn lunged forward with her weapon extended. Lightning quick, Elanor grabbed her crutch and thwacked the princess's arm aside. The dagger went skidding across the floor.

"Try again," Elanor said.

A welt appeared on Aislynn's wrist, but she said nothing as she retrieved the fallen knife. This time, her pose had some tension in it. But still, she wasn't fast enough and the dagger went flying out of her hand when the crutch cracked against her arm. Again and again, Aislynn attempted to attack Elanor, and each time she failed.

Despite the growing lump on her wrist, the princess fought on. And Elanor watched. Watched how she held herself, how she held the knife. Watched how she became more aware of her body and her weapon.

Aislynn's dagger clattered to the floor once again. On the bed, the fox opened one eye, yawned, and went back to sleep.

"Keep going," said Elanor, but this time when Aislynn bent down to pick up the knife, Elanor could see her hand shake. For a moment she thought of suggesting they stop, but Aislynn wrapped her fingers around the hilt and straightened, taking her position in front of Elanor once again. Her eyes were closed.

But instead of attacking, she just stood there, her breathing ragged and face bright with red blotches. Across the room, the flames in the forge crackled. It took a moment for Elanor to realize that she hadn't lit the fire.

"Aislynn—" she said hesitantly, reaching for her crutch.

The room exploded with magic.

A burst of flame and heat hit the ceiling. Aislynn's eyes flew open and she leaped back, releasing the dagger. But instead of falling to the floor, it shot across the room, heading directly toward Elanor.

Elanor threw herself against the floor as the knife whizzed over her head and buried itself in the wall. Aislynn had dropped to her knees, her wrists crossed over her chest.

The fire sputtered out, but magic hummed in the air.

Carefully Elanor sat up, wincing. Dagger was half-hidden beneath the pillow, her back haunches trembling.

"Shh, shh, shh," Elanor said, petting the fox until she stopped shaking.

"I'm sorry," Aislynn said, a look of horror on her ashen face. "I'm so sorry. I didn't mean to—I'm sorry."

Elanor reached up to pull the dagger from the wall. But it was buried deep and wouldn't budge. Looking back at Aislynn, Elanor gave her a small smile.

"I told you to attack me, didn't I?" She glanced down at her tender leg. "By all accounts this lesson appears to be a success."

Aislynn helped Elanor back to the infirmary, acting as an extra crutch as the two of them hobbled along the tunnel, leaving Dagger behind to sulk about her interrupted nap. Neither Elanor nor Aislynn, despite their best efforts, had been able to remove the dagger from the wall. Elanor assumed the same would apply to the scorch marks above the forge.

"Maybe we should start you on a bow and arrow," Elanor said. "Less chance you'll hurt yourself. Or others."

"I want to learn everything," Aislynn said earnestly. "I want to be helpful."

"You need to find the right way to use your abilities," said Elanor. "Your powers are no good to you if you can't control them."

"I know," the princess said. Her color had begun to return. "Tasmin has been helping me. And I'm hoping Dimia will teach me some healing spells. Maybe I'll even learn how to perform the slumber. It's just—" Aislynn took a deep breath. "I've spent my entire life believing that magic is dangerous and wrong. And even though I know that the Path lied to me, to all of us, I can still hear the voices of the advisers, of the headmistresses and teachers, telling me that there is wickedness growing inside of me. And a part of me still believes them." Her voice wavered. "I still say the prayers. I still think of self-cursing. I still fear what I can do." A tear slipped down her cheek.

Elanor was silent. She knew exactly how Aislynn felt. How it was possible to believe something so fully, so completely, that even when you knew it was a lie, it was still impossible to leave it behind. How there would always be doubt and fear and guilt.

"Not everything washes away" was the only thing she could think to say. "Sometimes, when you come out of the muck, no matter how hard you scrub, you'll never come away clean."

Chapter .15

Elanor's leg was re-bandaged and she was allowed, begrudgingly by Dimia, to sleep in her own bed. But that night her room seemed to be buzzing with magic, and unable to sleep, she headed toward the kitchen.

Still uneven on her crutches, she turned into the main entry and nearly fell over Aislynn, who was kneeling on the floor in front of the Four Sisters' altar. She looked a fright, her hair a black nest, eyes bleary and unfocused. When she stood, Elanor realized that she was wearing her dress backward.

"Aislynn?" she asked, but when the princess didn't answer, Elanor grabbed her sleeve and gave her a shake. The princess blinked as if she had just noticed her.

"I had a dream," said Aislynn. Her voice was far away.

"A dream?"

There were candles burning in the hands of each of the Four Sisters, indicating that some of the Orphans were out on patrol, and branches of pine lay at their feet, which meant that someone was honoring the memory of a loved one. These days it seemed that the altar was never bare.

"Thackery sang me their song," said Aislynn. "'The Ballad of the Four Sisters.'"

"I'm sorry," said Elanor, deeply confused. "He has a terrible voice."

Aislynn hummed a little of the familiar tune, missing a few of the notes. "It's a lovely song."

"It's a sad song." Elanor was unnerved by the princess's casual tone. "But soldiers love their tragedies."

"They're very different from the Four Sisters I know," said Aislynn. "Those sisters are a warning to us and not to be admired."

"It's not admiration; it's honor," Elanor corrected. Was this really the best time for a lesson on the Four Sisters? Both of them would likely benefit from going back to sleep. "Each of us has a sister we feel a special loyalty toward."

But Aislynn had stopped listening. She had that strange look in her eyes again, that dreamy gaze. She reached out for the statue of Sister Swan.

"Feathers," she said, and then, without warning, turned and headed toward the Mountain's entrance.

The stairs were complicated for Elanor but somehow she managed to follow the wayward princess. By the time she emerged from the hollowed-out tree, into the cold winter morning, she was afraid that she had lost Aislynn. But the princess was waiting for her, each exhale visible in the air.

Elanor tried to catch her breath. Sweat was forming on her lower back and along her neck. Despite that, she still shivered as an icy wind disturbed the trees. Her leg hurt, but it was the comforting ache of sore muscles, not the sharp pain of healing bone.

"We need to go past the barrier," said Aislynn.

"It's not safe." Elanor grabbed her. "We're unarmed."

Without a word, Aislynn lifted the hem of her skirt, revealing a set of knives strapped to her calf. It appeared the princess was adapting to life in the Mountain. She removed the daggers and passed one to Elanor, but not before Elanor noticed the large, dark welts on her leg.

"We're not going far," Aislynn said.

Even though it made her uneasy, Elanor followed Aislynn toward the barrier. She knew Thackery would never forgive her if the princess was hurt, or worse. It had snowed the night before, so maneuvering through the knee-high drifts was a challenge. Luckily Aislynn no longer appeared to be in a rush.

Instead, she seemed content to travel slowly, her eyes scanning the landscape carefully.

As they approached the barrier, Elanor reached out and placed her hand on Aislynn's shoulder so she could pass without confusion. Magic washed over them as they went through. Then, without warning, Aislynn darted into the icy drifts, headed toward something a few yards away. She knelt down in the snow.

Before Elanor could go after her, Aislynn was already on her way back. She was holding something in her arms, cradling it as though it were a child. A dress, made of green silk, its delicate beading glittering like the snow around them.

"I knew it would be here," Aislynn said, her expression grim.

"What is it?" asked Elanor.

"A ball gown," said Aislynn. "And there's blood on it."

They brought the dress back to the Mountain and took it to Tasmin. Thackery and Ioan were already in the kitchen when they arrived. When Thackery saw Aislynn, his long strides brought him to her side immediately.

"Where were you?" he asked, taking her face in his hands. "I woke and you were gone."

"I had a dream," said Aislynn, pink cheeked from the cold.

Thackery frowned. "I thought they had stopped."

"This was a new one," Aislynn said. "Different than the others."

"Why didn't you wake me?"

Tasmin passed out hot mugs of cider, and the princess, still clutching the bloodstained gown with one hand, took a long drink.

"I had to go to the altar first," she said. "I don't know why; I just had to."

"You found something?" Thackery looked down at the dress she was holding.

She nodded and handed him the mug. "It was out in the snow." Lifting up the dress, she revealed the dried bloodstain on the back. It looked fresh. There was a small slit in the fabric, which Tasmin poked with her finger.

"Looks like it was caused by a knife," she said.

"An ogre!" said Ioan. Everyone turned to stare at him.

Elanor sighed. Her leg hurt, and no longer in a good way. She made her way to a chair and fell heavily into it.

"There are no such things as ogres," she said. They were nothing but children's stories, passed down from parents who were long gone. "And this isn't the first ruined dress we've seen out here," she reminded him.

But it was the first one since Aislynn's arrival. And far closer to the barrier than any others.

"There's never been blood before," said Ioan, coming over to look at the dress.

"You heard Tasmin," said Elanor. "It was probably from a knife."

Ioan was unperturbed. "Maybe the ogres have knives for fingers?"

Elanor ignored him. There were feathers decorating the neckline of the gown. Most of them were gone, but a few downy fluffs, dyed green, remained. She looked over at Aislynn, who seemed interested in them, too.

"Feathers," she whispered, just as she had in front of Sister Swan. "I knew a girl who wore dresses like this." She glanced up at the others. "Violaine." Aislynn's face was stony. "But a lot of girls wear dresses like this." She looked over at Tasmin. "Someone is taking them." She touched a finger to the cut in the dress. It was along the arm, where it would wound but not kill. "Someone is taking them and hurting them. No," Aislynn corrected herself. "Hull. He's responsible. I know he is. He told me what he does to royal girls who stray."

"What about the mirror?" Elanor asked. "Have you learned anything else?"

Aislynn's hand went to her waist, where the bag with the mirror was still tied. "No," she said, frustration evident on her face. "I don't even know where to start."

"You said something about dreams," Elanor said.

"Yes." Aislynn put a hand to her forehead as if it ached. "They show me things."

Unsettled, Elanor exchanged a glance with Ioan. She had never heard of anyone having dreams like that. Only Tasmin didn't seem concerned.

"What kind of things?" asked Tasmin.

"I dreamed about Cinnamon, and about my parents' home," Aislynn said. "But last night, I dreamed about standing in the snow, in the same place I found the dress. I was wearing one of my old gowns, but it was red. I didn't realize the red was blood until I touched it."

The kitchen was silent, except for the crackling of the fire in the stove.

"I should go back," Aislynn said. "I might have missed something."

"We could check the forest," offered Thackery lamely. But they all knew that whoever had done this was long gone. That this dress was just another disturbing dead end.

Aislynn wasn't deterred. "I won't just sit around and wait for another dream," she said. "If there's something out there, I'm going to find it."

Chapter .16

It had taken a lot of convincing for Dimia to allow Elanor back on guard duty. But her injury was healing well, and there were few safer places than up in a tree near the edge of the barrier. The climb had been slightly daunting, but Elanor had gone slowly and was now sitting with her leg extended on one of the branches.

Then came the crunch of feet on snow. Quickly Elanor notched an arrow and aimed it down through the trees, the ground below visible. Whoever was coming would walk right through her line of sight. She held her breath as the footsteps came closer and faster.

Suddenly a wolf appeared. Rearing up, she placed her

paws on the tree trunk and stared straight up at Elanor, her tail wagging. There was reddish fur behind her ears. Cinnamon.

Elanor released the breath she had been holding. She returned the arrow to her quiver, slung her bow over her shoulder, and climbed down carefully. Joining the wolf at the foot of the tree were Brigid, Rhys, and others. The Orphans who had taken the villagers to the north had returned.

"Did we surprise you?" Brigid asked as Cinnamon made an excited circle around them.

"Completely," said Elanor.

"Liar," said Rhys. He nodded at her leg. "That looks better."

"Feels better, too," said Elanor. "Did you have any trouble on the way back?"

"If by trouble you mean huntsmen, then no," Rhys said. "We were lucky."

Elanor didn't think it was luck. The Queen's attention was elsewhere now.

"But if by trouble you mean the outrageous growling of this one's stomach"—Brigid poked Rhys in the side—"then yes, we had plenty of trouble."

"I can't help that I have a healthy appetite."

"A kind way to describe your gluttony," Brigid shot back.

"Ouch." Rhys clutched his chest. "Watch your aim."

Elanor rolled her eyes. "I'm sure we can find you something to eat," she said.

"That's all I ask," said Rhys, leaning down to give Cinnamon a good scratch on the neck. The wolf's back paw pounded on the ground, creating a small, powdery snowstorm.

"Before we fill his stomach," said Brigid, holding out her wrists, "I need to have these taken care of." She was still marked with Elderwood's custody spell.

"Looks like we both need to see Tasmin," said Rhys, draping his arm over Brigid's shoulders.

With a whistle Elanor alerted the other guards hidden throughout the trees that she would follow the others. She waited until she heard two short whistles in return before heading across the barrier and toward the Mountain with Rhys and Brigid. Cinnamon trotted behind them.

"Ioan and Thackery were placing bets to see if you'd ever come back. Ioan thought you might have gotten used to living in a palace," Elanor told Brigid.

The other girl snorted. "I'm sure he'd think that, since he's never lived in a palace. It's so . . ." She seemed to be searching for the word.

"Quiet," Elanor said at the exact same time Brigid did. They both laughed, but not out of amusement.

Josetta had always locked Elanor in at night. Even now

she could remember how many stones made up the wall in her bedroom and how many planks lined the floor. If she closed her eyes, she could still see every inch of that room.

Tasmin wasn't the only one waiting for them in the kitchen. Dagger was perched above the stove. When was the last time the little fox had seen an animal as big and powerful as Cinnamon? What would she do? Dagger climbed down the wall and slowly came to a surprised stop in front of the large wolf. Her nose twitched, and her head dipped to the side in confusion.

For her part, Cinnamon sat quietly and watched as the fox moved closer. First Dagger sniffed the large, snow-damp paws, then the tail and lower regions, all of which Cinnamon accepted with regal stoicism.

Then to Elanor's relief, Dagger positioned herself between Cinnamon's two front paws, stretching upward, nuzzling as much of the wolf's neck as she could reach. When the fox was done, Cinnamon slid gingerly to the floor. Dagger curled into a ball between Cinnamon's front paws, not even stirring when Cinnamon rested her head protectively over her body.

"Well," said Rhys, "that seemed to go well."

Elanor watched as Brigid gave her hands to Tasmin. Concentration was evident on Tasmin's face, from the deep line that formed between her eyes to the veins visible in her neck. Tasmin was quite powerful, so Elanor was surprised that the burst of magic, when it came, felt jagged and uneven, like broken glass.

"Are you all right?" asked Elanor once Tasmin had released Brigid. The cook looked pale and unsteady, but she refused Elanor's help.

"I'm fine," she said, looking at Brigid. "They've changed the spell. It's stronger."

"It felt different this time," Brigid confirmed. "More restrictive."

"It reminds me of—" Tasmin looked very worried.

"Reminds you of what?" asked Elanor.

"Reminds me of Josetta's custody spell," Tasmin finally said.

Elanor and Brigid exchanged a concerned look.

"That's impossible," said Brigid. "You removed it. Josetta's spell can't be removed."

"I said it reminded me of it. It's not the same spell, but there are similarities. Almost as if the royals are adapting her spell."

The possibility made Elanor ill. But how could that be? Josetta hated other royals as much as they hated her, and despite Cyril's urging, she had done her best to keep her "gift," as she called it, within her palace walls.

"They're so ungrateful," Josetta had fumed on numerous occasions.

"Of course they are, Your Majesty," Cyril would drawl. "It's for their own good, but you can't expect peasants to understand that."

"You're quite right, Cyril." The Queen had been eating another one of her lemon tarts, covered with sugared lemon slices. Elanor had been forced to test it, of course, and she could still taste the tartness on the back of her tongue.

"After all, 'a wolf raised in a barn may have food and warmth, but if the door is left unlatched, it will return to the forest it came from,'" Cyril intoned, a hand on his chest.

Josetta had thrown a lemon slice at him. "You toad, you know how I hate it when you quote *The Path* at me."

But Cyril had only grinned wickedly. "Their ideas aren't all bad," he had said. "In fact, I daresay, your beliefs align with most of them."

"Don't be silly," said the Queen, waving a hand in irritation. "I'll admit there is some truth in what the Path teaches, especially in regard to commoners. But this nonsense about how royal women should refrain from magic? Absurd."

"Not all women wield their powers as magnificently as you do, my dear," said Cyril.

"That much is clear," Josetta had sniffed, rearranging

the candlesticks on the table with obvious annoyance. "I've heard that most royals think I'm kidnapping their rebellious daughters, sending them threats and briar bushes. As if I would be interested in moody princesses who can't control their own powers."

"Rumors are nasty things," said Cyril, but Elanor had seen him smile.

"Amazing that they have time for such gossip. We both know the custody spell used for their household servants is woefully inadequate. Why doesn't the Path focus their attention on *that*?"

"How *are* your experiments going?" Cyril asked.

"Well enough." Josetta had taken another lemon slice from the top of the tart. "The last two attempts were . . . disappointing, but I think this new spell has promise."

"It will be quite the accomplishment if you perfect it." Cyril had leaned back against the couch, lacing his hands behind his head. He missed the way the Queen's eyes narrowed, but Elanor hadn't. She knew that look and shrank back against the wall.

"*If* I perfect it?" Josetta had asked, her voice sharp.

Cyril sat up immediately. "Not *if*, Your Majesty. I meant *when*. Of course I meant *when*."

"If you meant *when*, why didn't you say *when*?"

"I misspoke," Cyril bowed his head, his chin nearly touching his chest. "My foolish tongue got away from me."

"Then maybe you ought to hold that foolish tongue from now on," said Josetta, sneering. "I declare, Cyril, sometimes you're as pumpkin headed as a commoner." The Queen rose from her chair and swept from the room. Elanor had quickly followed, but not before seeing the look of utter hatred that crossed Cyril's face.

"I'm just grateful to have it removed," Brigid was saying now, taking a seat next to Elanor. "It's like having a part of you locked up in a tower . . ." Her voice trailed off.

Elanor didn't have to glance up to know that everyone was staring at her. Conversations about magic and the Queen usually meant someone would say something they regretted, and then everyone would look at Elanor to see if she had been hurt or offended.

But that kind of magic—that easy, natural magic—was something that had been taken away from Elanor before she had known what it was. What she felt was so faint that summoning it was painful and often embarrassing. Unlike the others, she didn't depend on it, didn't trust it. Sometimes Elanor wondered what was worse—never knowing exactly what you had lost, or longing for something you could never have again.

❤ ❤ ❤

It wasn't until they were heading toward the barracks that Elanor noticed just how exhausted Brigid appeared. And not exhausted in the way one was after a long journey, shoulders heavy and feet dragging. Brigid's weariness was all over her face, in the crease that had formed between her brows, in the downward turn of her mouth, in the tightness of her jaw.

"It's good to have you back," Elanor said.

Brigid smiled, but anyone could see it was forced. There were circles beneath her eyes and her brown skin was ashen.

"I need to speak to Aislynn," she said, but she let herself be led in the direction of the barracks.

"She's not here," said Elanor, explaining about the dress and how Thackery and Aislynn had gone to search for any clues. "Did you discover anything about the mirror?"

Brigid shook her head dully. "I discovered that Linnea is pregnant," she said.

That explained Brigid's appearance. Elanor took her friend's hand.

"I'm sorry," she said.

But Brigid shrugged her off. "It's my own fault. I know better than to fall in love with a princess."

Chapter .17

Matthias was carefully folding sheets when Elanor entered the infirmary. It was the first time she had seen him completely upright since bringing him into the Mountain. He was taller than she remembered. Dagger sat on his pillow licking her foot daintily.

"You seem better," said Elanor.

"I've been given permission to bathe myself today," he said with a grin. "It's embarrassing how excited I am to do so."

"It's a special kind of pleasure," said Elanor.

His smile grew and her pulse fluttered in her wrist.

"Has she been giving you any trouble?" she asked, nodding toward Dagger.

"Not at all." Matthias gave the little fox a gentle pat on the head. "Kept me from being lonely, actually." He nodded at Elanor's leg. "How are you feeling?"

"Better." She shifted her weight a little, testing the limb in question. "Glad to be on both feet again."

"It's frustrating being stuck in bed," said Matthias. "I think I've slept enough to last me my whole lifetime."

"Yes, well." Elanor glanced around the room. The healer was nowhere to be seen, and the rest of the beds were empty. "I had hoped to see Dimia, but since she's not here . . ." She was about to leave when Matthias stopped her.

"I was actually going to come looking for you," he said.

"Me?" There was that familiar twist in her stomach, that hot itch across her palms. His eyes were dark. Eager.

"My friends," Matthias said. "Bronwyn thinks they could be dead, but I know they're not." He rubbed the back of his neck. "I need you to train me," he said. "Like you're training the other girl."

"Aislynn," Elanor said, and Matthias nodded.

"I have to go back," he said. "I have to rescue my friends."

Elanor didn't know what to say. He was asking for a miracle. Training him was something she could do, of course. But what she couldn't do was help him rescue his friends. Getting Matthias and Ioan out of the palace had been dangerous enough. Trying to free a dozen prisoners, who might not even be in their cells? That was impossible.

The doubt must have been obvious on her face because he laughed.

"At least let me try to convince you over a meal," he said. "I'm starving. Are you?"

The dining cavern was crowded, filled with laughing Orphans and the scent of vegetable stew, hearty and sweet. Elanor had not realized how hungry she was until the bowl was in front of her. She dipped a chunk of bread into it, sopping up the thick stew, using the crisp crust as a spoon. Everything seemed to dissolve in her mouth, a savory mix of potatoes, celery, and carrots.

Her bowl was nearly empty before she thought to look up at Matthias. It appeared that he had not been lying about his appetite, for his dish was licked clean. He was looking across the room toward Rhys, who was standing near the entrance, talking to Brigid. Matthias was staring at the dagger attached to Rhys's belt. The beautiful curved dagger that had been—

"That's your dagger." Back in the forest, Rhys had taken the knife from a young man on a horse. "You're the soldier he took it from."

Matthias nodded.

"He's not going to give it back," said Elanor bluntly.

"I haven't asked for it."

"It's a well-made weapon." Elanor regarded Matthias seriously. "Can you even use it?"

"I can," replied Matthias, sounding indignant.

"We'll get you something else to use," said Elanor, realizing too late that she had just agreed to help him. He didn't seem to notice, though; his attention was still focused on Rhys. "Until then you should stop staring at it."

"It's not the dagger I'm staring at," he admitted, finally looking away. "It's the scabbard."

"The scabbard?" It was beautiful, even from this distance. Elanor remembered how she had admired the workmanship. Those perfect, even stitches in the leather, expertly shaped for the dagger. "Not much use for something like that without the weapon."

"My father made it," said Matthias. "He's dead."

"I see," said Elanor.

"It's the only thing I have left of him."

"And the dagger?"

"That was my mother's. I don't need it back."

"Unfortunately we've all got dead parents," Elanor said. "And no time to be sentimental."

Matthias shrugged. "It's like you said, what good's a scabbard without a weapon?"

Chapter .18

Having learned her lesson with Aislynn, Elanor began Matthias's training by giving him a rough wooden staff. Though it was large and unwieldy in the small confines of her room, she figured he would do less damage with it than if she gave him a sharper weapon.

From the stance he took, feet shoulder-width apart, posture straight, it was apparent that Matthias had some experience with weapons. After all, he had been armed when he and the rest of his party were ambushed by the Orphans. But it took only a few moments to discover that his skills were largely decorative.

Whirling her own staff smoothly, Elanor struck at him, aiming for his head. Though he was able to deflect her, he left the rest of his body exposed, a position she took advantage of. Matthias doubled over as her weapon made contact with his stomach.

"If that had been a sword, you would be dead," she told him.

"You were going to hit me in the skull!"

"Don't ever leave yourself exposed. Watch." Elanor swung her staff sideways so it protected her torso as well as her face. "Try it."

His face still scrunched up in pain, Matthias did as he was told and this time was able to deflect Elanor's attack. She chose not to acknowledge that she was moving exceptionally slowly. There was no point in discouraging him before they had even truly begun.

As they fought, she watched him carefully, just as she had done with Aislynn. He seemed to favor a formal style of fighting, and while it might have been effective in casual sparring, would be useless out in the field. Still, there was a grace to him, a comfort he had in his own skin that Elanor found appealing. More than once she had to remind herself that her observations were meant to help him become a better fighter, not for her own benefit.

Elanor compared her two pupils. Though Aislynn was lacking the fundamentals, they were strangely well matched. Perhaps that was a credit to the princess's stubbornness, but it didn't say much for the training Matthias had received. No Orphan would have been allowed out on a mission with his limited skills. Elanor couldn't help wondering how he had ended up as a part of that caravan.

After they had been at it for several hours, she finally asked. Matthias leaned back against the unlit forge, his brow damp and chest heaving.

"My mother," he said.

Elanor remembered how he had spoken of her earlier. The flatness, the bitterness in his voice was the same.

"She's always had ambitions for me that extended beyond my abilities." Matthias passed the staff from one hand to the next. "My father always deferred to her. When he died—" Matthias paused. "I used to be angry at her for sending me away."

"And now?"

"Now I'm angry at her for other things." Matthias looked at the floor.

Elanor spun her own staff in her hand, and as it slid against her fingers, she felt a sharp sting.

"Thorns!" she swore, and the weapon clattered to the floor.

Matthias came over as she lifted her hand to the light. Buried beneath the nail of her middle finger was a thick splinter.

Considering that she had recently seen her own leg

crushed and bloody, the sight of a tiny piece of wood piercing her skin shouldn't have made her woozy, but it did. Her knees and stomach wobbled, so she didn't brush off Matthias when he took her arm and helped her to the bed.

"I'm fine," she said, feeling immensely foolish.

But Matthias didn't seem to notice as he knelt in front of her, examining her finger carefully.

"It's not deep," he said.

"I'll be fine," she said again.

"I used to get splinters all the time when I was a child. My father taught me how to get them out." Matthias looked up at her. "May I?"

Elanor barely managed to nod before he placed his mouth around her finger. A jolt went through her, and she curled the fingers of her free hand around the edge of the bed. His tongue, warm and wet, felt its way along the edge of her nail. The dizziness she now felt had nothing to do with the injury. Then, his mouth clamped down and she felt the gentle drag of his teeth against her finger. He slowly withdrew his mouth, taking with it the pain.

Raising his head, Elanor could see that Matthias had his jaw clenched. Parting his lips, he plucked the splinter from between his teeth.

"Got it," he said.

Chapter .19

The next day there was a snowstorm. Most of the Orphans had gathered in the dining cavern to wait it out, and Elanor was surprised to see Wren among them.

Wren had not returned with the others after bringing the villagers north. Instead she had chosen to go on a patrol of her own. It was not the first time. From the snow caking her boots, it appeared as though she had just returned. She waved Elanor over.

"I'm working on a plan," Wren said after Elanor had taken a seat.

"A plan?"

"A new mission." It smelled as if she had been drinking. "A way to kill Josetta."

Elanor could only nod. They had tried, so many times over the years, to kill the Queen. They had even gotten close a few times. But Josetta had always retreated deeper into her palace, a fortress filled with huntsmen. And every time they had attempted to breach her walls, they had been tragically outnumbered. Most of the Orphans had accepted that the only way they could challenge the Queen was to make the expansion of her rule as difficult as possible.

But that had never been good enough for Wren, and Elanor could hardly blame her. Though they had both been kept prisoner in Josetta's castle for nearly five years, their experiences had been quite different. After that first day, where they had been lined up and evaluated like livestock, Elanor didn't see Wren for a long time. And when she finally did, she would spend many nights wishing she hadn't.

It had been during one of Cyril's visits. His custom was to come alone and dine privately with the Queen in her parlor before departing. This time, however, he'd brought someone with him: his son.

The boy was around Elanor's age, maybe a little older, and Elanor had been taken by how much he resembled his father. They both had that same pallid skin and dark hair, even sharing those pale gray eyes. Elanor barely heard him speak the entire visit.

"I had so hoped to introduce him to *your* son," Cyril had said to Josetta.

There had been no sign of the Queen's husband or her only child since Elanor's arrival. Sometimes she wondered if all that existed of the king and the prince were rumors.

"Benedict is not here," said Josetta, leading them down the hallway.

"I see." Cyril glanced back at his son, the annoyance clear on his face. "Well, perhaps you could tell us when he will be available next. My son is always in need of playmates."

But Josetta had seemed to ignore the barbed request, her step measured and quick as they headed to what Elanor knew was the Queen's private study, though she had never been allowed inside before.

"You're quite lucky, you know," said Josetta, slipping an ornate golden key into the lock. "I've just completed a very successful phase of my experiment."

The door swung open to reveal a nearly empty room. There was a fire roaring in the large fireplace and facing it, a dozen metal rings mounted to the stone wall. Four filthy young girls were chained to them with heavy iron shackles, and all but one turned away as Josetta approached them.

The rest of the room was spotless.

"Now, now," said the Queen. She reached for the girl who had not turned away. She flinched, and Josetta laughed. "I'm only here to show you off, you silly thing."

Josetta unlocked the girl's shackles and, chains in hand, pulled her to the center of the room. It was quiet except for the soft weeping of the other girls.

"Stop that," Josetta ordered, and the crying stopped, though Elanor could still see the tears dripping down their faces, catching the firelight before they fell.

"Your test subjects?" asked Cyril, moving closer to the girl at the center of the room. Her head was lowered, dirty hair blocking her face.

Elanor remained where she was, her feet taking root. She glanced over to find that Cyril's son was also frozen, the look on his face a mixture of fear, disgust, but worst of all, interest. When he noticed her watching him, he shot her a glare and moved forward to join his father.

"The work I've done on this one has been quite promising." Josetta grabbed the girl's hands. "Observe." Barely visible under the chains and the dirt caking her skin were two thin, red lines circling her wrists. "I still haven't figured out how to do it without the lines."

"Why wouldn't you want them?" asked Cyril. "They

make it so much easier to determine who has been restrained."

"I know," said Josetta, one long fingernail tracing the red line on the girl's skin. "I just hate the way it looks. I've been experimenting with that as well. Something more . . ."—she searched for the word—"interesting."

"Besides that, though, the spell is complete?" Cyril asked.

"Not quite." Josetta let the girl's hands drop. "I might have gone too far with this one. She can't use any magic at all." She sighed. "I want them to be able to perform *some* tasks." She wiped her hand on her gown. "After all, I already have enough male servants." She laughed and Cyril frowned.

"You're sure she can't do any magic?" he asked.

The Queen's expression darkened. "Of course I'm sure," she snapped. "Do you need me to prove it to you?" She huffed and pointed at Cyril's son. "Come here, boy," she ordered.

He did as he was told, visibly stiffening when Josetta draped her arms around him. "How old are you?" she purred.

"Thirteen, Your Majesty," he said haltingly.

"Thirteen, well." Her voice was low. "That's quite an exciting age, isn't it?"

Elanor could see him swallow.

"Yes, Your Majesty."

"I would like you to do something for me," said Josetta, her voice growing even quieter.

"Yes, Your Majesty."

"I want you to go over there, to that girl, and I want you to touch her."

Cyril's son jolted and turned to stare at the Queen. "Your Majesty?"

"I know she's dirty and unappealing, not to mention beneath you, but I need to prove something to your father."

The boy looked over at Cyril, who nodded.

"You heard your Queen."

"W-where do you want me to touch her?" the boy asked. The tone of his voice had gone from scared and startled to intrigued. Interested. Elanor's stomach twisted.

Josetta smiled and gave him a small push forward. "Wherever she doesn't want to be touched."

The boy took a few steps and looked over at Cyril, who nodded his approval. Squaring his shoulders, the boy moved to the middle of the room. The girl remained still. If not for the occasional breath, Elanor would have been convinced that she was a statue.

Reaching out a shaking hand, Cyril's son slowly and almost gently touched the girl's long mouse-brown hair. When she didn't stir, he ran his fingers down the length of it, stopping where it ended, near her hip. His hand hovered there for a moment and then, like a snake striking, he dug his fingers into the flesh of her upper thigh.

There was a sharp intake of air from the girl. Ignoring it, Cyril's son ran the back of his fingers up her body and this time when he grabbed for her, he got a handful of upper arm near her breast. Her pained yelp echoed in the enormous room.

"See," said Josetta proudly. "Instinct would have her using magic now, most likely to do something that would harm both your son and herself. Commoners have so little understanding of the elegance of magic. They think of it only in the most base manner."

"Quite good," Cyril said, still watching his son.

"I think I'll put her to work in the kitchen," Josetta mused. "After all, there isn't much more I can do with her here."

Elanor felt like a statue herself, standing there immobile as Cyril's son took a fistful of the servant girl's hair and forced her head back, her face now visible in the firelight. It was the last time Elanor saw Wren cry.

"Looks like someone wasn't lucky enough to miss the storm," Wren said, glancing past Elanor. Aislynn and Thackery were standing in the entryway, looking sodden and sullen.

"I'm not even sure what we were following," said Thackery once they had all gathered in the kitchen, Dagger watching them from her shelf above the stove. "There were several sets of tracks in the snow near where we found the dress, but they didn't make sense."

"What do you mean?" asked Brigid.

"There were two sets of footprints leading up to the dress, but only one set leading away."

"Maybe the first person was carrying the second?" Rhys offered, but Thackery shook his head.

"The indentations didn't get any deeper heading away. There was no added weight. And the only other prints nearby were definitely not human."

"But you followed them," said Elanor.

Aislynn nodded. "The original footprints seemed to be heading back out of the woods, but the storm hit before we could find out where they led. We had to abandon the search to return to safety. Obviously there won't be anything remaining once the snow stops."

Everyone sat in silence for a moment, the frustration palpable. Aislynn kept fidgeting, her leg bouncing up and down, disturbing Cinnamon, who had been attempting to use her knee as a pillow.

"Something else was strange," said Thackery. "There was no blood."

"No blood?" asked Brigid.

"The dress had a large bloodstain on it," Aislynn

explained. "A cut in the gown and lots of blood on the fabric. It looked fresh. But there was nothing in the snow."

"Did you dig for it?" asked Elanor. "Whoever stabbed Violaine, or whoever it was, could have covered it."

"There was nothing," said Thackery. "Besides the footsteps, the ground was undisturbed. No sign of anything being buried. We dug anyway. Nothing."

Silence settled around the table once again, this time interrupted by Aislynn, who slammed her fist so hard that it sounded as if she might have broken something.

"There has to be a clue out there that we can follow," she said. "Something that can help us."

Elanor said nothing, watching everyone's shoulders slump with resignation. No one knew better than the Orphans that you couldn't find something that didn't leave a trail.

Chapter .20

The room was warm, the mead was warm, and Elanor was warm. She held out her empty mug to Brigid, who made a sound somewhere between a giggle and hiccup before filling it to the top with the honeyed wine. Elanor leaned back against the wall and watched as Aislynn pawed at the buttons on her dress with one hand while gripping her own mead-filled mug in the other.

"I need help," the princess finally said, her arm dropping heavily to her side. "I don't remember these being so complicated."

"Here—" Brigid put down the bottle of wine and walked unsteadily over to Aislynn. She lifted her hand, palm facing the buttons, and closed her eyes. It took a few moments, and when Elanor felt magic in the room, it was as wobbly as Brigid. But when Brigid lowered her hand, the buttons were all in their correct buttonholes.

"Well done," said Elanor, lifting her mug in a toast.

Brigid curtsied.

They had been in Elanor's room all day, preparing for the evening ahead. The mead had been Brigid's idea. At first both Elanor and Aislynn had taken only a sip, but it tasted so good and felt so nice that Elanor had stopped resisting each time Brigid attempted to fill her cup.

The snow from the storm had melted quickly, which meant that winter was coming to an end. Heck, Ioan, and the others would be leaving soon. It was Tasmin who had suggested the ceremonies, a bonding one for her son and Heck and an initiation for Aislynn. There were few reasons to celebrate in the Mountain, so the idea had been met with great excitement. Everyone was grateful for a distraction.

Across the room, Brigid was very carefully lining her eyes with soot from the fireplace, miraculously not getting any on her yellow-and-gray dress. Her soft, curly hair was pulled back from her face with a bright matching ribbon, and her lips were painted a deep purple. Aislynn, in a green dress with a beanstalk embroidered near the hem, was attempting to braid her own hair and having the same kind of luck she had encountered with her buttons. It was clear this was the princess's first time imbibing mead.

Elanor pushed herself off the bed. "Let me," she said, confronting the mess that Aislynn had created. Carefully she unbraided the thick hair, using her fingers to undo some of the larger knots that had formed. As Elanor twisted Aislynn's hair together, Brigid regaled both of them with tales of her previous conquests.

"There was an Academy last year where I managed to get the attention of both a princess *and* her fairy godmother," she said. Clearly the mead had pushed Linnea out of Brigid's thoughts. At least for the time being.

"How is that possible?" asked Aislynn, trying to turn toward Brigid. Elanor placed a hand on the top of her head, forcing her to look forward. "Every fairy godmother's loving heart is removed when she takes her vows."

"You of all people should know there are ways around that," said Brigid, refilling her mug. "Something I'm sure Thackery is most grateful for."

"I didn't do it on purpose," Aislynn said, blushing. "It just happened."

Brigid leaned forward, sloshing some of her mead onto the floor. "And you never wondered how?"

"I just thought there was something wrong with me."

"Oh, Aislynn," said Brigid, and at the same time Elanor muttered, "Better not tell Thackery."

Brigid shook her head at Elanor and came over to stand in front of the two of them. "It's not that uncommon."

"You're not special," Elanor added bluntly.

"I never thought I was." Aislynn twisted her head to glare at Elanor. The untied braid slipped from Elanor's fingers. She threw up her hands and went to retrieve her mug.

"It's a self-fulfilling spell," Brigid explained, moving to finish Aislynn's hair. "The more you believe it, the stronger it is." She grinned, knotting a green ribbon at the end of the braid. "And I've convinced quite a few of your peers to put their faith in something else."

"You royals are far too uptight about such things," said Elanor, falling back on her bed.

She was wearing her favorite trousers and a red tunic that laced up the front. Her arms were exposed, displaying the beautiful decorations that Brigid had painted on her skin with shimmering ink. Though Brigid had drawn mostly patterns, there were a few tiny foxes hidden among the swirls and curls of gold. Even Cinnamon and Dagger, who were napping together on the floor, were dressed for the party, wearing blue ribbons around their necks.

"And you aren't?" asked Brigid, coming to sit next to Elanor. "I've seen the way Matthias looks at you, yet you've done nothing."

Heat rose in Elanor's cheeks, and she quickly focused her attention on the mug in her hands.

"He likes you," said Aislynn, joining them on the bed. "And he's rather handsome."

"Something else you might not want to tell Thackery," said Elanor, but Aislynn just stuck her tongue out at her.

"I think you like him, too."

"Of course I like Thackery," said Elanor, but she couldn't hide her smile. Matthias *was* handsome.

Brigid leaned her head back against the wall. "I can't remember the last time you liked someone."

"Not all of us spend our summers in palaces full of gorgeous princesses," Elanor reminded her.

"I'm sure we can change that if it's princesses you're interested in. But"—Brigid wiggled her eyebrows suggestively at Elanor—"why not take advantage of the fact that you've got a perfectly handsome, formerly concussed young man who appears smitten with you?"

"Ha," said Elanor.

"You like princesses?" The look on Aislynn's face spoke to her confusion. "And Matthias?"

"I like who I like," said Elanor. "Same as Heck."

"I didn't mean anything by it," said Aislynn, blushing. "I've just never met anyone like that before."

"Of course you have," said Elanor. "You think there aren't royals like us? Your people are just too concerned with blood and family lines to let people love who they love."

There was silence as Elanor took a long gulp of mead.

"They're not my people anymore," Aislynn finally said. "Not after tonight."

"I'll drink to that," said Brigid, and the three girls tapped their mugs together.

Chapter .21

The enormous room was completely open to the sky, except for the tangle of vines and curling leaves that formed a natural roof above them. The walls were lined with candles and mirrors, light thrown about the cavern in glittering patterns. Everyone had gathered to celebrate, and the room was buzzing with conversation and excitement.

A circle had formed in the center, where Tasmin stood. She wore a long robe draped over her shoulders. It was embroidered with a fox, wolf, swan, and owl, sewn with such care that they seemed to be observing the goings-on. A square had been drawn in chalk on the stone floor. It, too, was decorated with drawings of the four sacred creatures, one at each corner.

Elanor caught Matthias's eye. His gaze swept over her, across her bare arms and unbound hair. Even though the effects of the mead had largely worn off, Elanor felt dizzy and hot.

There was a hush. Elanor turned just as the crowd parted, revealing Heck and Ioan, their hands entwined. Both were dressed in black, Ioan in his favorite cloak, Heck in a tunic embroidered with golden thread, his wooden leg giving his gait a slight stiffness. Following them was Aislynn in her green dress. They all took slow, even steps to the center of the cavern and stopped beneath the canopy of vines.

"Welcome, all," said Tasmin, smiling. "And good evening."

"Good evening." The room echoed with the bright response.

"We are here to welcome one as our own. Aislynn." Tasmin extended her hand toward the princess, who came forward to stand inside the chalk square. "Do you pledge to honor the Four Sisters? To act with strength, cunning, bravery, and grace in their names?"

"I do," said Aislynn, her head lowered.

"Have you chosen a sister to pledge your loyalty toward?"

"I have." Aislynn's voice was steady. "I have chosen Sister Wolf." She turned to face the corner where the wolf had been drawn on the stone floor and bowed her head.

"Sister Wolf." Tasmin beckoned the others who had pledged to that same sister to step forward. Wren and Thackery, with Cinnamon at his side, were among them. "Do you accept this child as one of your own?"

"We do."

Tasmin placed four fingers on Aislynn's forehead. "Our lives are now entwined with yours." Magic pulsed around them, strong and steady before one last burst that settled over the entire group. There was a moment of silence, and Tasmin embraced Aislynn. "Happy hunting," she said.

"Happy hunting," everyone cheered.

Tasmin gestured for Aislynn to join the circle. She did so, standing next to Thackery, who eagerly took her hand in his as Cinnamon leaned against her leg. They smiled at each other, their faces glowing.

"We are also here to bless the bond of others," Tasmin continued. Heck's young daughter, Hedra, approached and clutched Tasmin's hand tightly. The little girl looked nervous. "We are here for Heck and Ioan. To celebrate their love."

Elanor's brother stepped forward, his fingers tightly linked with Heck's.

"And we are also here for Hedra. To celebrate her family." Tasmin's voice was strong in the massive room. "To bond people together requires a powerful spell," she said. "But it is also a misunderstood spell. Most believe its strength is a reflection of the woman who performs it. That is incorrect. The spell is only as powerful as the love shared between those taking the vow. And the love between Heck and Ioan is indeed a powerful one." Tasmin placed her palm over Ioan's and Heck's entwined fingers. "It is my honor to bond these two together."

They had closed their eyes and leaned forward until their foreheads were touching.

"Sister Swan, these two have pledged themselves to each other in your name. We ask only that you honor their love as they honor yours. That they may serve you and your sisters together in life and in faraway death. Now repeat after me," said Tasmin. "I pledge my devotion."

"I pledge my devotion." Ioan's and Heck's voices echoed after Tasmin's.

"And all my strength."

"And all my strength."

"To protect and care for you."

"To protect and care for you."

"Bonded for ever after in your love."

"Bonded for ever after in your love."

A jolt of magic caused a ripple of laughter from the crowd. Tasmin waved a hand and everyone quieted. "Hedra, please step forward."

Ioan and Heck lifted their joined hands and welcomed Hedra. Ioan lifted her into his arms.

"There is no greater bond than that of family," Tasmin said. "And no greater adventure than the one you will embark on together. Sister Fox and Sister Swan, we ask that you welcome these three into your hearts as they have welcomed you into theirs. Heck and Hedra, do you accept Ioan as your family? To care for him and love him without hesitation or boundary?"

"We do," they said in unison. Hedra practically shouted the words, her voice high and sweet.

"And Ioan, do you accept Hedra and Heck as your family? To care for them and love them without hesitation or boundary?"

Ioan's voice was clear and strong. "I do."

Tasmin turned to the others. "Do you promise to protect and honor this family?"

"We do" came the reply.

"Then I declare you a family, for ever after." With a smile, Tasmin flooded the cavern with magic as the crowd raised their voices in joyful cheers.

Chapter .22

Elanor heard a fiddle being tuned, and soon the stone walls echoed with its twangy plucking. Most of the crowd had spread to the edges of the cavern, giving a wide berth to the dancers who had gathered in the center. Couples were spinning and laughing, clapping their hands and stomping their feet as the room overflowed with music.

Brigid came through the crowd, a mug in each hand. "Thirsty?" she asked, passing Elanor the warm cider.

"Thank you." Elanor inhaled the cinnamon-scented steam hovering over the cup.

Both girls faced the dance floor, where Ioan and Heck were swaying together slowly, completely disregarding the fast tempo of the music. They looked so happy. And for the first time in a while, Elanor felt the same.

"Would either of you enjoy a spin around the dance floor?" Rhys joined them, hand outstretched.

"I can never say no to a handsome gentleman," said Brigid, placing her cider aside.

"I'll let you know when one shows up," said Rhys, swatting at Brigid when she pinched him. "Careful, that's my spinning arm." He winked at Elanor. "I'm coming for you next."

"I can't wait," she said, lifting her drink to them with a smile.

They spun away and disappeared into the throng of dancers. Elanor wrapped her hands around her mug and took a long sip. Above her, through the canopy of vines and leaves, she could just barely glimpse the stars twinkling in the dark. The air smelled like winter and snow, but she knew that it would be a clear sky tonight.

Her skin tingled from the magic floating in the air. The cavern was full of laughter and music and people swinging their partners in dizzying circles around the dance floor. Rhys and Brigid flew by, their hands linked. Across the room, Aislynn and Thackery were dancing, too, but neither seemed to be able to find the right place to put their hands or their feet. Finally Thackery took Aislynn's hands, clasped them around his neck, and put his own fingers around her waist. Elanor could see him mouthing "*one*, two, three, *one*, two, three" as they attempted a strange offbeat waltz. Both couldn't stop smiling.

They swayed by Matthias, who was against the far wall with his own mug in hand. When he caught Elanor's gaze, he lifted the mug in acknowledgment. Elanor did the same with hers, taking a long drink, not caring that she was no longer thirsty. The candlelight cast a warm yellow glow over half his face, the other half lost in the shadows. He was very handsome. There it was, that uptick in her breathing, that skip of her pulse. He was nice to look at and Elanor didn't want to look away. Why should she?

Elanor wanted to be touched. She could still feel the warmth of his mouth around her finger, the touch of his hand against her wrist. She finished her cider and returned the mug to one of the tables. Then she crossed the room, keeping her eyes on Matthias. He didn't blink.

"Would you like to dance?" she asked as she approached him.

He set aside his own drink and reached out for her. "I would be honored."

But they were as awkward as Aislynn and Thackery had been, both unsure. He tried to take her waist and one of her hands, while she attempted to hold his shoulders. Finally Elanor did exactly what Thackery had done. She placed both of his hands on her waist and linked her fingers behind his neck.

"There," she said.

"Thank you." He was blushing.

Elanor began to guide him around the floor, pushing his shoulder with her forearms to direct him where to go. After a few missteps he fell into rhythm with her. They moved to the slow twang of the music, neither of them saying anything.

Then she glanced up and her breath caught. He was staring at her, his gaze dark and intense. They stopped dancing and stood there, at the edge of the dance floor, looking at each other. Her skin was hot, her stomach doing somersaults all the way up into her chest.

"Come with me," she said.

Her room was dark, so Elanor lit a candle, the dim light revealing Matthias hovering in the doorway. Then he looked up at her. His eyes were two flames, flickering and warm.

Without a word, she took his hand and pulled him over to her.

The only way to reach him was to stand on her toes, so she did, and he leaned down and their lips met somewhere in the middle. He tasted like cider, like hot spice and sugar.

Elanor wrapped her arms around his waist and pulled him closer. His fingers tangled in her hair, holding it as if he was testing its weight. She slid her hands underneath his shirt, up his back. His muscles were tense but beginning to relax.

His shirt had to be removed. She wasn't quite tall enough to get it over his head without some awkward reaching, but she managed just fine in the end. She moved her hands over his bare skin as if she was smoothing out her bed linens.

Matthias seemed to lose his breath with each touch, sucking in air through his nose and holding it as if he had forgotten it was still there. Elanor stood on the very tops of her toes and whispered in his ear: "Breathe."

The breath he released was like a small storm, fluttering over her eyelashes and cheeks.

"Don't be nervous," she said.

"I can't help it." He looked thoroughly embarrassed. "I don't know what I'm doing."

Elanor didn't mind. She took his hand and put it where it felt good. He had nice hands. Soft. Warm. He kissed her and seemed less nervous. He touched her and his hand did not shake. She was no longer drunk, but everything felt hazy and slow. She liked the feeling. A warmth built in her stomach, pulling tighter and tighter until she could barely breathe, and then it released, like an arrow from a bow, and she fell forward, shuddering onto his shoulder. He kissed her again. Smiling, Elanor lowered them both to the bed.

Chapter .23

It was not long after that the thaw came. The change in weather brought a new energy to the Mountain. Despite the chill in the air and the stubborn patches of snow that clung to the ground, the world seemed ready to start anew. The scent of fresh dirt and green grass followed Elanor everywhere, settling on her clothes and skin like a wonderful perfume.

There was possibility in everything, and the Orphans seemed invigorated. Aislynn and Thackery returned to the forest to search for clues that might lead them to some answers about the gown or the mirror. Brigid hid her heartache over Linnea behind mindless chores, while Wren threw herself into the secretive plan she was concocting to kill the Queen.

With the thaw, it also came time for Ioan and the others to leave the Mountain.

"You said good-bye to Tasmin?" asked Elanor. Standing with Ioan in the entryway, she could already feel him slipping away. On the ground, Dagger seemed to feel the same, winding and rubbing against Ioan's legs. Stooping, Elanor gathered the fox in her arms, grateful to have something to hold on to.

Ioan nodded and patted his stomach. "She said good-bye the way she could, by feeding me enough food for a dozen people."

"You'll miss her food in Nepeta," Elanor told him, Dagger's fur warm against her fingers. They were going to join the others at Aislynn's family home. It was safe there. Even though he was her older brother, Elanor still felt responsible for him. Still wanted to protect him.

"It's not the only thing I'll miss," said Ioan. "Take care of yourself, all right?"

"I always do," said Elanor, holding Dagger close.

"You know what I mean." Ioan gave her shoulder a squeeze. "Sometimes it's not enough just staying alive." She knew he wanted her to come with him, but he did not ask, and she was grateful for that.

"Your family's waiting for you," said Elanor. If he stayed much longer, she'd start to cry.

Ioan nodded. "I'll see you soon," he said.

"You will," said Elanor, hoping it was the truth.

He pulled her into his arms and she let herself relax, just for a moment, in his embrace. Dagger squirmed a little between them, causing Ioan to release them both. Immediately Elanor missed him.

"I love you," he said.

Elanor wanted to say it, but she couldn't. It was just too hard. But the look on his face told her that he knew.

"Happy hunting," she said, and then he was gone.

It took an afternoon in the forge, smashing broken swords and melting down knives, before Elanor could face other people again. Even so, she felt uncomfortably raw, like a freshly peeled onion, as she entered the dining cavern. Already the Mountain felt empty without Ioan.

She spotted something unusual across the room: Matthias seated at a table with Wren. His eyes lit up and he gestured her over.

"I was just telling Wren what an excellent trainer you are," he said when Elanor reached them. She felt better just looking at him, at his wide, easy smile. Sometimes he seemed so untouched by all this darkness around them, all the death and destruction that Josetta had caused. He was so quick to laugh, so eager to be happy.

Elanor felt a twinge of jealousy. Could she have been this carefree if the Queen hadn't crossed her path? Could there have been a world, a life for her, where she felt joy every day instead of dread? Instead of fear?

"We're going to need all the extra hands we can get," said Wren. "And you couldn't have found a better teacher. She's a brave one, our Elanor."

Elanor's face went hot, but it wasn't out of embarrassment over Wren's uncharacteristic compliment. It was out of guilt.

Wren leaned toward Matthias conspiratorially. "Did you know that she risked her own life to bring an end to the Wicked Queen's?"

"I failed," said Elanor needlessly, but Wren ignored her.

"Both of us were prisoners in the palace when we were children," said Wren. "But Elanor was Josetta's favorite. A fact we attempted to use to our advantage."

Elanor longed to walk away, but her feet felt as heavy as the stone beneath them. Elanor and Wren had been prisoners for five years when the attempt on Queen Josetta's life was made. Wren had been sixteen, Elanor twelve.

That morning Josetta had received a letter, one that Elanor later learned had informed the Queen of her husband's murder. Even now, Elanor could not understand how a woman who so hated commoners would marry and have a child with one. But at the news of his death, Josetta had draped a black shawl over her head and shattered all her mirrors. Somehow the Queen had cared for him.

"I'll kill them all," she had told Elanor. "They have no honor. Only animals would kill one of their own in such a way."

No Orphan ever took responsibility for his death. Even today some claimed that Josetta had killed her husband herself or had arranged to have him killed to rally her followers against the rebels. If that had been her intent, then the Queen had succeeded, for the Midlands grew rapidly in the years following the murder.

But that day, Josetta had mourned and eaten so many sugared lemons that Elanor was sure she could no longer taste them. Still, Elanor returned to the kitchen again and again to refill the Queen's plate. It was the first time since she had arrived at the palace that she was allowed to go on her own. Josetta's grief had loosened the leash, if only for a day.

Late in the afternoon Elanor had found the kitchen deserted. She let herself into the pantry but quickly retreated once she discovered she wasn't alone. Wren said nothing when she emerged, followed by Cyril, who Elanor knew had been summoned to the Queen's side.

"Are those for Her Majesty?" asked Cyril, straightening his collar. He pointed to the tray in Elanor's hands.

"Yes, sir." Elanor curtsied obediently.

"I'll take them," he said, grabbing the plate of tart candied slices. "Please remain here until you are summoned." Cyril left, leaving Elanor alone with Wren.

The other girl had brushed past her but said nothing as she began putting away the clean dishes stacked next to the sink. Elanor just stood there, unsure what to do with this freedom. Finally everything had been put away and still Elanor waited, expecting the other girl to leave. But she hadn't.

"Do you miss them?" Wren had asked quietly. When Elanor only stared, she asked again, "Do you miss your family?"

Elanor had nodded, but it was a lie. She didn't remember her family. Not after all these years. She didn't remember anything outside of these walls, outside of the world Josetta had created for her.

"We can go home." Wren's voice was barely audible. She approached Elanor, coming close. Too close. She smelled like overripe fruit, too sweet and on the verge of rot. Elanor was used to Josetta's scent, the fresh, clean smell of lemons.

"I need your help," Wren said, and Elanor was reminded of their time together in the prison, all those years ago. How scared she had been and how Wren had not cried, not once.

Elanor had looked into Wren's eager, desperate eyes. And Elanor had wanted to help her. So she nodded. A look of relief swept across Wren's face and her hand dove into her pocket. She pressed a small, smooth object into Elanor's palm.

"When you take the Queen her tea tonight, pour this into the cup."

Elanor had uncurled her fingers. There was a glass vial in her palm. It was filled with pale green liquid.

"A sip will only make you sleepy. The whole thing will kill you." Wren's eyes were wide and desperate. "You have to do it tonight," she said. "They're coming to save us."

The next time Elanor had seen Wren, they were safely in the Mountain. Many people had been killed during that failed attempt on Josetta's life, but they had both been rescued. From then on, the girl that Elanor remembered from the palace was gone. Wren transformed herself, cutting her hair and finding someone to make it the brilliant blond she now preferred. She had Gideon cover almost every inch of her skin in ink and trained until she was stronger than anyone else in the Mountain.

"But Josetta discovered the poison," Wren said, finishing the story, bringing Elanor back from her memories. "And forced Elanor to drink it. She was nearly dead by the time the others found her."

"Like I said," muttered Elanor. "I failed."

"You were a child," said Wren.

"There's no excuse."

"It sounds like you were very brave," said Matthias, reminding Elanor that he was still there. His eyes were filled with a myriad of emotions. But all she could see was pity.

Elanor looked away. She could feel the burn of the poison as if she was swallowing it all over again.

Chapter .24

He was going to need a weapon. There were plenty to spare, of course, but Elanor didn't want to give him just any sword or knife. Every warrior deserved something that was meaningful, that was important. Even though she didn't remember them, she carried her parents on her back. Her father's quiver and her mother's bow with a scrap from one of Tasmin's aprons tied to the end.

They had never failed her.

And Matthias already had a meaningful weapon. At least, part of it.

"I only need the scabbard," she told Rhys, who tried to wave her away. Usually he was much more generous after dinner, but so far she had been unable to convince him to make the trade. She held out the pieces of leather she had gotten from Dimia by swapping the black salt Gideon had traded, which she had exchanged for a new blade. "I'll make you a new one."

Rhys wrinkled his nose in confusion. "But what good is it without the dagger?" he asked, his hand going protectively to his side, where she could see the jeweled handle peeping out of the leather scabbard.

"I can make a new dagger." She shook the leather scraps at him again. "And I'll make you a new sheath."

"Your leatherworking isn't nearly as good as your blacksmithing," he said.

"So I'll ask Brigid to make you a new one," said Elanor, trying to rack her mind for something she could swap with Brigid. "It's a fair trade."

"Hardly!" Rhys laughed. "You still haven't told me why you want it."

Elanor frowned. "I want to give it to Matthias. His father made it."

Understanding crossed Rhys's face. "Aha." He unbuckled his belt to remove the scabbard. "You should have just told me," he said, handing it over.

Elanor ran her fingers over the soft leather, examining it carefully. Making a dagger to fit this unusually shaped scabbard would be difficult. Usually the case was made to suit the weapon, not the other way around. But she was up for the challenge.

"Thank you."

"Yeah, yeah." He snatched the pieces of leather from her. "You're also doing patrol duty for me for the next week."

Elanor spent several days on the dagger. She had to scrap her first two attempts completely. When she finally got the correct curve of the blade on the third try, she made it too small to fit the sheath properly. It wasn't until her fourth attempt that she managed to make a knife that was the right size and shape. She had to repurpose the handle from another weapon, and it was a little too big, but she thought it might be better for Matthias's long fingers. The important thing was that it fit the scabbard, and it did. It fit it perfectly.

Elanor gave him the dagger first.

"It's beautiful," he said, holding it carefully in his open palm.

"A soldier is only as good as his weapon," she said, pleased that he liked it. She pulled the scabbard out from behind her back. "And a weapon is only as good as its sheath."

Matthias stared at it for a moment. "It's— But—" He

looked up at Elanor, surprise on his face. "How? Why?"

Elanor shrugged. She didn't really know why she had worked so hard to get it for him.

"Thank you," he said. He put the dagger and sheath aside and stood. "Thank you," he said again, leaning down.

She reached up, her lips finding his. Elanor kissed him deeply, her hands fumbling for the buttons on his shirt.

Afterward they lay there, the fire casting warm shadows across their bodies. Elanor rested her cheek against his chest, while his fingers traced the tattoos across her shoulder. His skin was so smooth, and she was suddenly aware of all the marks on her body. How had he lived in this world and remained so untouched? She pulled away, suddenly self-conscious, something she had never felt before.

"What's wrong?" he asked, sitting up.

"I've never seen anyone like you before," she said. "Your skin, your hands. Everything is so soft."

"I wasn't a soldier for very long," he said, clearly uncomfortable. He pulled the sheet up to cover his chest. "Haven't had a chance to develop calluses yet."

Elanor looked at her own rough and scarred hands. She reminded herself that each mark had been well earned. When she looked back at Matthias, she saw that he had been watching her. Waiting. She leaned forward and kissed him. He reached up to take her face in his hands.

Elanor recoiled and Matthias froze.

"I'm sorry," he said, eyes wide.

"No." Elanor shook her head, trying to get rid of the sick feeling in her stomach, the crawling sensation against her skin. "I—I just don't like having my face touched," she said.

"I understand," said Matthias, his body stiff.

"No you don't," she said. And suddenly, inexplicably, she was furious at him, with his gentle hands and his unmarked skin. What did he know about scars? About memories you couldn't shake, even after all these years? "Look at you. You've never been hurt, not really."

Her words hung in the air between them like a curse. Like a wall of thorns.

"I lied to you," he finally said, his head lowered so she couldn't see his eyes.

"What?" The word was a gasp.

"When I first came here, I said that I had never seen the Queen." His voice was quiet and steady, but pained. "I have seen her. She was the one who gave me this." He twisted away from Elanor.

On his shoulder, a part of his body she had not yet explored, a mark had been burned into his flesh. Only this one was unlike any brand Elanor had ever seen. There was no symbol, just a blackened circle.

"My father brought me to her," he said. "I was a boy. She asked if I was loyal to her." He took a deep breath. "She was a stranger to me, but I knew what my father wanted me to say. So I said yes. She asked me if I would wear that loyalty. And I said yes."

Elanor closed her eyes, remembering her own branding. The fire had been so hot, and the brand glowing and red, its shape distorted and muted by the flames.

"I chose this for you," Josetta had said, pulling the iron from the fire. Her voice had dropped to a whisper. "It will be how I know you." But Elanor hadn't understood, not until she felt the heat. Not until she felt the press of the iron against her back, heard her own skin blacken. And as she smelled her flesh burn, she heard Josetta's voice.

"May you be protected from the wickedness inside you. May you be guarded from your own power."

Elanor had felt heat spread through her, as if her entire body was on fire, her heart at the center, burning as red and hot as the end of the brand. She wanted to scream, but there was no breath in her lungs, no voice in her throat. She was no longer part of her body; she had escaped it and was far away, Josetta's words the only thing connecting her to the earth.

"The pain makes it real, my pet," Josetta had whispered, bringing her back, placing her again in her skin, in a body forever altered, forever ruined. "It will make you remember."

Matthias retrieved his shirt and slipped it over his head. "I may not have the same scars as you and the others, but I know what it's like to be hurt." He glanced over at the forge, at his gift. The dagger and the scabbard. His father's scabbard. "Your parents died trying to save you from the Queen. Mine gave me to her."

Guilt burned Elanor's throat, but she said nothing and took his hand. They sat in silence, watching the fire go out.

Chapter .25

The first time Elanor had found Matthias and Wren sharing a table, heads together, she thought nothing of it. But the second time sent a twinge of apprehension up her spine. Wren was a solitary person, and though she was sometimes seen with Gideon or Bronwyn, she seemed to prefer being on her own. She certainly didn't spend time with people like Matthias.

But there they were again, Wren doing most of the talking and Matthias carefully listening. They didn't even notice Elanor until she was standing right in front of them.

"Elanor!" said Wren in an uncharacteristically chipper tone. "Just the person I wanted to see." She pulled back a chair, and Elanor took a hesitant seat. "We've been discussing the details of my newest mission."

All apprehension disappeared, and Elanor leaned forward eagerly. She had been hoping to talk to Wren about this exact thing. She wanted to volunteer. She had failed in her attempt to assassinate the Queen the first time. Now she had an opportunity to make things right. To do what she should have done all those years ago.

"Poison," said Wren dramatically.

"Poison?" Elanor repeated. How was that Wren's newest plan? That was an old plan. One that had failed miserably. One that had cost Wren's parents, and several others, their lives.

"We're going to poison the castle's water supply." Wren continued, oblivious to Elanor's dismay.

"What? How?"

"We'll go in through the tunnel—the same one you used to rescue Ioan and Matthias. The prison guards should be easy to dispatch and strip of their uniforms. Then we'll make our way to the well and pour the same potion we gave you into the water supply. It will put everyone in the castle to sleep."

"But not Josetta. She'll have someone testing her food and water," Elanor reminded her. "When everyone starts falling asleep, she'll know something is wrong."

"I'm counting on it," said Wren, her eyes intense. "I

don't want the poison to kill her. I want to do that myself."
She smiled. "Once most of the guards and servants are
incapacitated, we'll unlock the gates and attack. The Wicked
Queen and her army in one fell swoop."

Wren sat back, satisfaction written all over her face.

It was a good plan. A dangerous plan, but a good one.

"When do we leave?" asked Elanor, eager to get started.

Wren blinked at her before exchanging a look with
Matthias.

"Matthias and I will be delivering the poison," said
Wren.

There was a buzzing in Elanor's ears. Surely she had heard
her incorrectly. Wren was taking Matthias with her? A half-
trained novice who had just been given his first real weapon?
Someone who wasn't even pledged to the Orphans? That's
who Wren was trusting with this mission?

"I don't understand," she said.

"He volunteered," said Wren, as if that explained her
decision to choose him.

"It's the only way I can rescue my friends," said Matthias.
"I can get them out while we poison the others."

"Elanor, you can join the group that will be waiting
outside the castle gate," said Wren. "Not everyone will fall
asleep. We'll need Orphans to pick off the survivors."

Elanor could not speak. Her mouth was dry, her skin clammy.

"Elanor—" said Matthias, reaching out for her.

"I have to go," she said, standing.

"It will all be over soon," she heard Wren call as she walked away.

Elanor went to the kitchen, but she wasn't hungry. In fact, she wasn't anything. She was in shock. How could Wren do this to her? A terrible thought stilled her steps. Did Wren know the truth? Had she discovered that Elanor had been lying all these years about what had happened in Josetta's bedchamber?

The heat of the stove barely registered to Elanor when she sat down next to it. Quickly Dagger extracted herself from the shelf where she had been napping, her soft paws making barely a sound as she padded across the floor and into Elanor's lap. Tasmin was chopping vegetables, her knife a blur against the bright orange of the carrots and the brilliant green of the celery.

Perhaps this was her punishment, Elanor imagined, smoothing out Dagger's tail, the fur both soft and coarse under her palm. The thought made her sick, but she couldn't deny that she deserved it. She could have ended it all with that vial of poison. She could have stopped the years of death and grief that followed.

But that just proved that Josetta was her responsibility. She wasn't going to let Wren or Matthias take on the wickedness that she should have destroyed. This was her battle.

"I know about the plan," Elanor said.

"I see." Tasmin looked away.

"You're the one making the poison, aren't you?" If anyone in the Mountain knew how to brew something that could sicken a palace full of people, it would be Tasmin. She wasn't a soldier, but she was a fighter.

Tasmin let out a small huff of a laugh and nodded at the pots on the stove. "I can tell you're disappointed that Wren didn't choose you to go with her." She glanced at Elanor. "You think it's a good idea?"

"Perhaps," said Elanor, though as she began thinking back over Wren's strategy, she realized that it was not just a dangerous mission, it was suicide. Dagger nudged at her stilled hand, and Elanor resumed the petting.

"It's reckless," Tasmin said. "A martyr's plan."

"There are worse things to sacrifice yourself for," said Elanor, thinking of her conversation with Heck months ago.

"There are better things to live for," said Tasmin, stirring the soup.

"Then why are you making the poison for Wren?" asked Elanor. "If the plan is so dangerous, so ill planned, why are you helping?"

"Because Wren would find a way no matter what I did," said Tasmin, putting aside her spoon. "I made the poison for her under one condition. That she wouldn't take you with her."

Elanor stared at her for a moment before the reality of what Tasmin had said sank in. The relief that came from realizing that Wren had not discovered her secret was immediately replaced by anger.

"I don't want you to get hurt," said Tasmin.

Elanor couldn't feel her fingers, her face, Dagger's fur— anything. How could Tasmin have betrayed her this way? "It's not your place to protect me."

Tasmin laughed, but without mirth. "If anything is my place, it is that."

"You had no right."

"You don't owe anyone anything," said Tasmin, laying a hand on Elanor's shoulder.

"Don't I?" Elanor shook her off. There were some things that Tasmin couldn't understand. She didn't live in Elanor's skin, didn't remember what she remembered. She didn't know what it was like.

"People didn't sacrifice their lives so you could do the same. Your life is worth more than this."

"It's my choice, Tasmin," said Elanor. "Mine." She stood, Dagger tumbling awkwardly from her lap. The fox yowled from the floor before scurrying back to her shelf.

Even though it was her fault, Elanor glared at Tasmin. "And I don't need you or anyone telling me what my life is worth." Without another look at her mother, Elanor left the kitchen and its warmth and safety and went to get her weapons. The debt she owed was finally going to be paid.

Chapter .26

Elanor made sure to keep a good distance behind Wren and Matthias. As she walked, she became more and more angry. The numbness was gone. All she had time for now was anger. Anger was good. Anger was powerful.

They were making excellent time. Finally they reached the thorn wall. Ducking behind a tree, Elanor watched as Wren took out her sword and hacked an enormous hole into the tangle of brambles. Clearly she had no interest in hiding their place of entry.

Once they were through, Elanor moved closer, keeping to the other side of the thick briars. Peering through the twisted thicket, she watched as Wren found the swath of camouflage that was hiding the hole. It looked smaller than Elanor remembered, and she shuddered, thinking of how cramped and dark it would be in there.

Matthias barely hesitated before he crawled in. Elanor waited for Wren to do the same. Instead she just stood there. Suddenly she turned and looked behind her. Elanor had just enough time to drop to the ground near the thick tangle of roots. When she glanced up, Wren was gone.

Elanor scanned the forest through the thorns, but she couldn't see Wren. She was just about to venture out when Wren came into view, dragging an enormous log. The veins in her neck throbbing, she leaned the entire weight of the wood against the entrance, effectively blocking the tunnel. Elanor watched as she did this several times, building a sturdy blockade with fallen tree trunks and large rocks. There was no possible way for anyone to come back out of the tunnel.

With a smile, Wren wiped the sweat from her face and turned away. Elanor had hardly any time to get out of sight before the other girl came sauntering through the briar wall, whistling as she headed off in the direction of the Mountain.

For a moment Elanor found herself staring at Wren's retreating figure. What was going on? Where was Wren going? What had she done?

It was a suicide mission, but it seemed that Wren had never intended to follow through with it. She had sent Matthias in alone and blocked his exit, giving him and those he was attempting to save no chance of getting out.

Sprinting through the brambles, toward the tunnel, Elanor rushed to deconstruct Wren's wall, straining against the heavy rocks and logs that had been piled against the tunnel's entrance. She wasn't as strong as Wren, and it took her twice as long to undo the work, her muscles aching. Was Matthias near, waiting for Wren to follow? Or had he gone ahead, hoping that she would catch up with him?

Either way he was in the prison, behind Josetta's walls, alone. Elanor reached into the dark entrance, her fingers finding the soft, wet dirt of the tunnel. If she reached in far enough, her entire hand disappeared in the darkness. Quickly she pulled her arm back, trembling. She knew what was on the other side. She knew what waited for her there.

Elanor looked up at the sky, hoping that the Four Sisters were watching over her. With a last prayer, she crawled into the tunnel. On her hands and knees she fit, but the darkness terrified her. Lifting her head was impossible, so she kept her chin tucked against her chest, eyes straining and seeing nothing. Her weapons kept brushing against the top of the tunnel, sending dirt into her hair and down her shirt. The earth was soft around her, smelling of rain and grass, but it wasn't comforting. It filled her throat and she had to remind herself to take small, even breaths.

The tunnel seemed to go on forever, and Elanor began to fear that there was no end to it, that she was trapped in the blackness and the damp, like a princess buried in a glass coffin. When she finally reached the end, her skin was slick with sweat and her heart was racing. She waited for her eyes to adjust, quietly brushing dirt from her hands and neck. There was the faintest candlelight flickering down one of the corridors. She headed toward it, careful to place her feet gently between the debris spread across the ground.

After walking for a little while, she heard voices up ahead. Guards? It was all whispers and she could barely make out what was being said. She crept closer, hoping she'd be able to figure out who it was and what they were talking about before they noticed her.

"Has there been any word?"

"No, sir." The second voice was very weak. Sir?

"Have they questioned you?"

"No, no one has asked us anything."

Elanor crept closer. She could see a figure ahead of her, hands pressed up against one of the cell doors. It had to be

Matthias. Why wasn't he freeing them? And why was he being called sir?

"Has there been any news of Matthias?" he asked.

Elanor froze, doubt curling in her stomach like a beanstalk vine.

"No, sir. We haven't seen him since the day we arrived."

"Do you think he's still alive?"

Elanor couldn't hear the reply, but whatever it was, it was enough for Matthias, or whoever he was, to nod.

"I'll be back for you soon," he said, and headed toward what seemed to be the dungeon exit.

Silently Elanor followed, her hand on her ax. She had only made it a few steps when someone in one of the cells called out in a hoarse voice.

"Benedict, there's someone behind you!"

Elanor saw Matthias reach for his knife, *her* knife, but she was too fast. She had her blade against his throat before he could lift his weapon. The dagger clattered to the floor.

"Pick it up," she snarled.

He did and when he straightened, he was greeted by a slap across the cheek.

"That's for lying to me," she hissed through her teeth. "Benedict."

"Elanor, I meant to—"

"Now is not the time for apologies," she snapped. "You can leave with me now and explain yourself, or you can die without telling me the truth."

Before he could answer, Elanor heard a low rumble of laughter.

"What have we here? Two trespassers, I see."

Out of the darkness came two huntsmen, with their weapons drawn. Elanor froze. They had been caught.

Chapter .27

"Let's take them to the Queen, shall we?" One of the huntsmen had an arrow aimed straight at Elanor's heart. She glared at him.

"Looks like she's eager to meet Her Majesty," the second huntsman said. Both wore Josetta's symbol on their chests. Once they had all been the same, all commoners, all looking for a life of freedom, but these men had given it up for three meals a day and a roof over their heads.

"What's this?" One had noticed the pouch strapped to Matthias's chest.

"It's wine," said Elanor, hoping they'd take a long swig.

"Is it?" He punctured the bag with his knife. From the

sound that Matthias made, it seemed that he had pressed quite hard.

Elanor could do nothing as the poison gushed onto the floor.

"Come on."

She was dragged out of the dungeon, Matthias at her side. She struggled, but it was no use; the minute they were in the light, it was clear that they were outnumbered. Every huntsman in the courtyard was focused solely on them.

Strangely, Matthias didn't seem very worried or upset. Instead he looked almost relieved. He walked freely, not even trying to resist the grip of the soldier who was leading the way, hand clamped around Matthias's arm.

Elanor did her best to be as difficult as possible. She dragged her feet and let her body go limp, so the huntsman eventually had to lift her up and carry her. That was when she started wriggling and biting. Finally the other huntsman put his knife against Matthias's throat.

"You'll walk," he said, "or we carry him. Once we've emptied him of his blood."

Elanor walked.

They were led across the courtyard and into the palace. It had been so long since Elanor had been inside, but she had not forgotten. She was ashamed to feel a twinge of nostalgia, as if she had actually missed the walls that had imprisoned her.

But while it was familiar, there was something strange about it as well. Josetta was a woman of particular tastes, someone who wanted everything to be just so. She did not abide things being out of place, or any sort of mess or untidiness.

Which is why Elanor was shocked to find the whole palace in a state of disrepair. It might not have been obvious to anyone seeing it for the first time, but Elanor knew how the Queen preferred things, and the unkempt nature of the rooms they passed through would never have been allowed when Elanor lived there. Indeed, she had been punished more than once for not returning items to their correct locations.

Everything was covered in a thin layer of dust; the furniture was moth-eaten and frayed. Some of the carpets were bunched up or crooked, while there were several paintings hanging askew on the walls.

They were taken toward the throne room, and Elanor steeled herself, preparing to come to face-to-face with the woman, the monster, she had escaped all those years ago.

But when the doors opened, it was Cyril standing on the dais. He hadn't changed much in the past five years, although he had more wrinkles and more gray in his hair. Seated to his left was another man, whom Elanor recognized as his son. He had lost the small amount of childhood softness that had been evident on his face the last time Elanor had seen him, that terrible night in Josetta's private study. Now he looked nearly identical to his father, with his pale skin, dark hair, and viciously sharp cheekbones.

Cyril smiled as they entered. "Welcome," he said. "I've been expecting you." He glanced at the guards lining the walls. "Take their weapons," he ordered.

As the huntsmen stripped them down, Elanor noticed that Cyril's eyes remained fixated on what was being taken from Matthias. No, not Matthias. Benedict. His sword, his bow, the arrows, and the dagger she had made him. Cyril watched eagerly and smiled when the weapons were brought to him.

"Where is Matthias?" Benedict demanded.

Cyril laughed, his eyebrows raised. "Asking about your decoy first? Surprising. I would have expected you would want to see your mother immediately."

Elanor's throat went dry. "His mother?"

Cyril's eyes seemed to gleam as his gaze shifted to her. If he recognized her, he made no indication. His wide smile was directed more at Benedict than at her.

"You didn't know, did you? Oh, this is wonderful. It appears that introductions are in order." Cyril made a dramatic bow. "Allow me to introduce you to Prince Benedict, the only son of Queen Josetta."

Chapter . 28

For a moment Elanor thought she had gone blind. The room flashed white and she stumbled, held up only by the huntsman's firm grip on the back of her shirt. No. It couldn't be.

Benedict was more than just a liar, he was a traitor, and he was the son of the woman who had ruined Elanor's life, had branded her and her family. The woman who had killed her parents.

Her vision snapped back into focus. This was the reason he had been so eager to return to the palace, so willing to take on Wren's mission—he wanted to get back, wanted to get back to his mother.

Anger churned in Elanor's chest. For the first time in years, she felt magic building inside her, powerful and raw. It shocked her. There was no need to summon or hope for it to appear; it was just there, a part of her that had been sleeping now reawakened.

"Elanor—" Benedict the liar said, and that was enough.

Elanor lunged forward, magic burning her palms, her hands on fire. "I'll kill you," she snarled, but before she could reach him, she was knocked to the floor by one of the huntsmen. It took two of them to keep her there. Inside, the magic retreated, returning to its hiding place.

"Now, now, my dear," said Cyril, shaking his head. "That's no way to treat your future leader."

Elanor spat at his feet. "He'll never be my leader."

"Very well." Cyril smiled and gestured to his guards. "Take her away."

The ground was wet and cold in the cell they flung her into. Before she could scramble to her feet, the door slammed closed and the guards took off down the corridor, their laughter echoing behind them.

Elanor wrapped her fingers around the bars in the door and rested her head against the iron. When her temper had cooled to a boil, she began to assess her situation. The cell was enormous and there was a small window. It was a little too high for her to see out of, but when she stood on her toes, she could see the sky and the tops of buildings. She wasn't in the dungeons. She was in one of the towers.

Suddenly there came a sound from outside. Elanor rushed back to the cell door, expecting to find that the guards had returned, but no one approached. The noise came again. A woman's laugh. Tired and weak, but familiar.

She heard the drag of fabric across the floor, as well as the sound of metal. Straining to look through the small window in the door, Elanor discovered another cell across from hers; this one was more open, with floor-to-ceiling bars.

A woman was standing there, in a long satin dress, her red hair shimmering in the pale light. She took a step closer, and Elanor could hear the clank of chains beneath the hem of her gown.

"Hello, pet," Josetta said.

Chapter .29

Her last night in the palace, Elanor had brought Josetta her tea. The poison heavy in her pocket. Elanor stopped just outside the door and, balancing the tray in her arms, took out the vial and removed the stopper. The green liquid smelled of apples and smoke. It left no trace when poured into the cup of tea. Hands shaking, Elanor knocked upon the Queen's door.

"Come in," called Josetta. When Elanor entered the bedchamber, the Queen was sitting at her dressing table in a beautiful robe, cloudlike curls spread across her shoulders. Looking over at Elanor, she smiled.

"Come here, child," she said, beckoning. Carefully

Elanor placed the tea tray on the table and went to stand near the Queen. "Closer," Josetta said, and laughed when Elanor took the smallest step she could muster. "Closer, my pet." She reached out a hand, garnished in jewels, and grabbed Elanor's wrist. "I won't bite," she said as she pulled Elanor into her lap.

The Queen smelled like lemons. She ran her fingers through Elanor's hair. Her nails were long and sharp against Elanor's scalp, but there was something comforting about the gesture. Something familiar. Had her mother brushed her hair when she was a child? Elanor could not remember her mother. Not anymore.

"What lovely dark locks you have, my dear," said Josetta.

There was an expectant silence.

"Th-thank you, Your Majesty," said Elanor obediently.

"Such charming freckles." A nail slid down Elanor's nose. "And what pale skin." The same finger danced across Elanor's cheek. "You may grow up to be quite the beauty, my little pet." Josetta's fingers were gentle against Elanor's face. They were the softest thing she had ever felt.

"I have a gift for you," said the Queen. "It's on the bed."

It was a gown, red and satin, like the one Josetta wore.

"Put it on."

Elanor had never worn anything so beautiful. Even though it felt slippery and her feet tangled in the hem, she loved it. It made her feel elegant and special and not at all like the others. Not at all like Wren.

"Let me help you with the back," said Josetta, taking the laces in her hands and pulling them tight. "Take a deep breath, pet." Elanor could barely contain her gasp as air was chased from her lungs.

"Look at you," Josetta had said, turning her toward the mirror. "You could be mistaken for a royal."

Elanor could still remember how she had blushed, her breathlessness forgotten.

"Well." Josetta ran her hand through Elanor's locks again. "Not with your hair like this." She leaned forward, pressing her cheek against Elanor's. "Would you like me to comb it?"

"Yes, Your Majesty," said Elanor, hardly able to believe what was happening. Perhaps Josetta truly cared and saw something wonderful in her. Perhaps she saw that Elanor was not like the other peasants, that she was unique. Special.

Josetta gestured for Elanor to sit, and the comb she retrieved was the same one that Elanor used to untangle the Queen's hair every evening. It was silver, with needlelike teeth that gleamed in the firelight and the image of a harp imprinted on the handle.

It felt wonderful, the slide of silver against her skin, the smooth strokes through her long hair. But then Josetta pushed a little harder, pulled a little more fiercely. Elanor bit her tongue. Because even though it hurt, she didn't want Josetta to stop. The silver teeth scratched her scalp and soon something wet crept down Elanor's ear. She looked up at the mirror and saw a tiny trickle of blood running down her neck. Josetta tied Elanor's hair in a red ribbon.

"Now then," said the Queen, "I think it's time for tea."

Elanor stood and went to retrieve the tea, which had surely gone cold by now. Perhaps the Queen would send the tray away and ask for another. But no, it was still hot to the touch. Hands shaking, Elanor went to the Queen, who was now perched on her bed, the luxurious linens and pillows piled around her like a snowy mountain.

"You look quite lovely," Josetta said.

"Thank you," whispered Elanor, the teacup clanking in its saucer. She raised the tea to her lips. She remembered what Wren had said, that one sip would do nothing but put her to sleep. That drinking the whole cup would kill her. Elanor took a sip, waiting for the taste of apples, but there was nothing but the tang of the lemon that Josetta preferred.

"Tell me, pet," said Josetta. "Do you love me?"

"Yes," said Elanor, surprising herself.

Josetta laughed, the sound more marvelous and magical than anything Elanor had ever heard. Of course she loved the

Queen. Josetta had taken care of her all these years. Fed her, protected her. Given her this beautiful dress. Combed her hair. She was all that Elanor had.

The Queen leaned forward and ran her fingers down the side of Elanor's face. "And I love you," said Josetta, her gaze unwavering. "Now drink, my precious pet."

Without hesitation, Elanor lifted the cup to her lips and drank every drop.

"Good girl." Josetta rose from the bed and took the empty cup from Elanor's fingers. "You've done so well."

Elanor was tired. So tired. Her eyes and head felt as heavy as gold. She sank into the warmth of the mattress, into down feather pillows and smooth silk sheets. The Queen's face hovered above, her beautiful face, surrounded by a crown of red curls. Elanor's eyes refused to stay open.

"Do you love me?" Josetta asked again, tightening the blankets around her.

"Yes," said Elanor. Her throat had begun to burn. "Yes."

Chapter 30

Elanor pushed herself into the corner of her cell and pulled her knees up to her chest. She didn't want to look at the Queen, didn't want to hear her. She wanted to disappear, to turn to stone in this frozen, forgotten room. But Josetta would not stop.

"I know you've missed me, my dear." The Queen's voice floated through the cold, stale air of the cell. "Just as I have missed you." There was the muffled clank of chains again. "Have you been a good girl these past years? Or have you become like all the others?"

The wall was ice against Elanor's back.

"I thought you would understand." The Queen's voice

had an edge of irritation to it now, one that Elanor remembered well. "I was protecting you, pet. You think your life is better out there? Here you were safe. Safe from the world, from the others, from yourself. There's something inside of you, wild and vicious. Monstrous."

That brought Elanor to her feet.

"You have no idea how monstrous I can be," she snarled through the barred window in the door, wishing she could break through and wrap her hands around the Queen's pale neck.

"I took such good care of you," said Josetta, as if Elanor had not even spoken. "Did I mean nothing to you?"

"Nothing," whispered Elanor, but it was a lie. How badly she wished that it were the truth. Wished that this woman were a stranger to her, that she felt nothing but hatred toward her. But she didn't. Beneath it all there was the horrible twist of tenderness.

Josetta tilted her head, as if surprised at Elanor's response.

"Was I not a mother to you?" she asked. "You were like a child to me."

"I've met your child," said Elanor. "And we are nothing alike."

For the first time Josetta looked startled. "That's impossible."

"Your son. Benedict," said Elanor, firing each word like an arrow through the bars. "He's here, in the palace. But you must know that."

Josetta's face went white, parchment white. "No." Her fingers were tight around the bars of her own cell. "No. I don't believe you."

"Fine," said Elanor. She ached, her head vibrating like an anvil.

"Elanor."

It was the first time the Queen had ever spoken her name.

"You have to save us," the Queen's voice was small. Childlike. Fear sat like a mask upon her features, making her almost unrecognizable. "If they have Benedict, you have to save him. Please."

This Queen was not the one Elanor knew. Josetta was never afraid, never in need, never begged. It made Elanor sick. All she wanted to do was hate this woman, but all she could think of was how sweet and bitter those lemon tarts had been. And how much Josetta had loved them.

"I hate you," she whispered through the bars.

"If only you could," said Josetta. "You'll always love me, and that's your curse. I'm a part of you, my pet. I'm burned into your heart."

Chapter 31

Two huntsmen marched down the hallway.

"No!" said Josetta, her voice low and urgent. "Don't let them take you, pet!"

But one of the guards was already unlocking Elanor's door. She was too surprised to react when they pulled her out of the cell.

"You're free to go," said one of the huntsmen.

"What?" Elanor could not believe what she was hearing.

"The prince arranged for your release."

"No!" cried Josetta. "Don't go. Stay with me. Stay with me!"

One of the guards slammed the flat of his sword against the bars of the Queen's cell.

"Quiet!" he bellowed.

Josetta shrank back into the dark, too far for Elanor to catch another glimpse before she was led away. The Queen she knew would never be cowed by a servant. What had happened to her?

The huntsmen took her through the deteriorating castle, across the dusty courtyard, and practically shoved her outside, slamming the gate behind her. Elanor was frozen there on the ground, her hands and knees caked with melted snow and mud, shock and confusion swirling through her.

She had been released. But why?

Elanor made her way through the forest in a fog. There must have been some mistake. How could they have let her go?

She focused on putting one foot in front of the other, and when she felt the familiar hum of magic she looked up. The sun was about to rise, Tasmin would be out soon to re-charm the barrier. Elanor was nearly home.

She was numb. From the cold, from everything. She didn't even react when Rhys dropped from a tree in front of her and grabbed her arms.

"You're back! You're alive!" he said joyously, but all the happiness dropped from his face when he saw her expression. "What happened? Where's Matthias?"

Elanor blinked.

"Ellie? Elanor!" Rhys shook her a little. "Are you all right? What happened?"

She tilted her head, still confused. "They let me go," she said, still not understanding it herself. "They let me go."

There was a pile of food in front of her and a wall of concerned faces, but Elanor could do nothing but stare at her hands. All around her, the rest of the Orphans seemed to be celebrating something, but Elanor wanted nothing more than to sleep. Forget.

"What happened?" asked Rhys for the hundredth time.

"Where's Matthias?" asked Brigid.

"He wasn't Matthias," Elanor managed, each syllable painful. "He was Benedict. He wasn't a prisoner, he wasn't a commoner. He was a prince. He *is* a prince. Our prince."

"What are you talking about?" asked Thackery.

"He's Josetta's son," said Elanor, spitting the words out as if they tasted bitter. Because they did. The truth was a horrible, bitter thing. "He lied to us."

There had been plenty of warning signs. If she had been more careful, more aware, she would have known that Benedict wasn't who he said he was. In fact, a part of her wasn't even surprised. But before she could admit this to her friends,

Wren strode over to the table, an unpleasant smile turning up the corners of her mouth.

"Where have you been?" she asked.

Something in Elanor snapped. Wren. It was Wren who had led Benedict to the castle. Wren who had meant to lock him inside, to leave him there. Had Wren known she was returning the crown prince to his palace? Elanor remembered how calm Benedict had seemed when they were led to the throne room, how willingly he had gone. Had they planned this, the two of them? Had Wren known? The thought of Benedict sharing his secret with Wren made Elanor ill. She stood abruptly, her chair clattering to the floor as she grabbed the front of Wren's shirt.

"What have you done?" she asked, her voice harsh.

Wren pulled back in disgust, untangling Elanor's hands from her tunic. "You should be thanking me," she said.

"Thanking you?" Elanor could only stare at Wren in disbelief. "Did you know who he was?"

"He was a traitor," Wren said.

"He was the prince."

"What?" A smile still adorned Wren's face.

"He was the prince!" Elanor screamed. "Josetta's son! You just returned the Queen's son, her only heir, back to the palace!"

The entire room was silent.

Wren's face went white. "You're lying," she said. "He was in prison. Why would Josetta have her own son in prison?"

"I don't know!" Elanor said, her head aching.

"No," said Wren, her hands in front of her like a shield. "You're lying."

"Something is wrong," said Elanor, turning to Rhys and the others who were still sitting at the table. "Josetta said—"

Wren grabbed her shoulder, spinning her around.

"Josetta said?" Wren repeated. "You saw the Wicked Queen?" Before Elanor could answer, Wren laughed, the sound like a bitter gasp. "Of course. She's still got her claws in you, hasn't she? Whatever she says you believe, don't you? You're still nothing more than her little toy, her little pet." Wren leaned in closer, her voice dropping to a whisper. "I know the truth," she said, clutching Elanor's arm. "I know what happened that night."

Elanor could barely focus—everything seemed too bright, too sharp. She tried to sit, but Wren's grip only tightened.

"Do they know?" Wren turned to face the others, her voice echoing in the silence. "Do they know that you never gave Josetta the poison? That *you* drank it, Elanor? You drank it to save her."

And there it was. The truth. There was a sharp intake of

air around her, like a whistle in her ears. Elanor shrank back in shame, guilt burning her throat. She wanted to say something. The faces around her reflected shock and pity. She wanted to explain.

"You're a traitor and a liar, Elanor," sneered Wren. "Just like your little—"

Suddenly she was on the ground. Everything happened so quickly. It had been quiet and then, all of a sudden, it wasn't. Someone started screaming, and Elanor was jerked forward by her shirt.

"Where is it?" the huntsman roared.

Elanor could only blink at him. This wasn't real. This wasn't happening. She was in the Mountain, wasn't she? The Mountain was safe.

With a snort of disgust, the huntsman tossed Elanor aside, and she hit the table, rolled off, and smacked the floor hard. She didn't feel any of it.

What finally shook her into reality was the bloodcurdling cry. Rhys. Her heart pounding in her throat, she pulled herself off the ground.

He was bent over at the waist, clutching his face, blood pouring from between his hands.

"Give it to me or I'll take the other one!" The huntsman's knife was shiny with blood.

"Rhys!" Elanor cried just as the soldier plunged his sword down. He missed Rhys's face, but the blade sliced into Rhys's shoulder and he let out another agonized scream, his knees buckling. The soldier pulled something from Rhys's body and shoved him aside.

"I've got it!" the huntsman called to the others, his smile both triumphant and terrible.

Elanor scrambled to Rhys. Dropping to her knees, she pressed her hands against his bleeding shoulder. The blood was hot beneath her fingers. His own hands were still cupped over his injured face.

"I'm sorry, I'm sorry, I'm sorry," she said, forgetting for a moment that she had just put herself, exposed and weapons still sheathed, in the midst of an attack. But when she looked up, the huntsmen were gone.

It was pandemonium. All around were the moans of the injured, of people crying out in pain. Where were the others? Thackery. Brigid. Aislynn. They had been right next to her, hadn't they? Rhys's body was heavy in her arms.

"Help!" Elanor managed to find her voice. "Someone help me!"

"Elanor!" Aislynn emerged from the throng of bodies and blood, rushing over to them. Her cheeks were smeared with soot, her hair singed, but she seemed unharmed.

"Heal him!" Elanor's voice seemed to belong to someone else, someone far away.

Aislynn fell to her knees beside them, a greenish tint to her skin. For a moment it looked as if she might be sick, but she swallowed harshly and lifted her palms. "Where?"

Elanor almost snapped at the dumb question, but she looked down and realized that they were both so covered in blood that it was impossible to tell.

"His shoulder and"—Elanor's stomach rolled—"and his eye. They cut out his eye."

"Move!" Aislynn ordered, but there was no bite in her words.

"I can't," said Elanor, her voice cracking. She was afraid to move, afraid to spill more of his blood.

Taking a deep breath, Aislynn placed her shaking hands over Elanor's and closed her eyes. The warmth of magic tickled Elanor's fingers. Underneath her palm she could feel the wound close and heat return to Rhys's body. With a gasp he regained consciousness. And started screaming.

Elanor jerked away in shock, falling back onto the cold stone floor. Quickly Aislynn placed her palm on Rhys's forehead. The screaming stopped as he slumped back into a safe unconsciousness.

"I put him in the slumber." Aislynn moved her hand to

his mutilated eye socket and the hot pulse of magic hovered in the air for a moment. "I can only heal the wound," she said. Elanor gave her a shaky nod. They both knew there were some things that magic couldn't repair.

"We'll need to move him to a bed." Sweat glistened on Aislynn's forehead and her breathing was ragged, but she was calm. Nothing like the girl Elanor had met in the woods all those months ago. "Just watch him for now. Make him comfortable if you can." She paused. "Maybe make him a bandage so it won't be so jarring when he wakes up."

Elanor nodded and began tearing off a strip of cloth from her shirt.

"He'll be all right," said Aislynn.

No he won't, Elanor wanted to say, but she knew if she said anything, she would start to cry.

The first thing she did was place the makeshift bandage over Rhys's face, covering the tender skin. Then she stretched him out onto his back and ripped his bloody tunic away from the healing wound on his shoulder.

Then she looked up.

The room was a mess. Tables and chairs were upended and strewn all over, food smeared across everything. Two still forms were laid out on the ground, their faces covered. Thackery was only a few feet away, leaning his head back against the stone map as Aislynn knelt on the floor, healing his injured leg. Next to him was Brigid, face in her hands and shoulders trembling. Everyone seemed to be in shock, the sound of crying filling the room. Blood was all over the floor.

What had happened?

Elanor felt sick. This was her home. How had they found them? After all these years . . .

They must have followed her. It was the only way she could account for the huntsmen's sudden and miraculous discovery of the one place the Orphans had kept hidden for so long. She must have led them right to her friends and family. This was her fault.

Chapter 32

The Mountain was in chaos. The attack had been so swift and so brutal that no one knew exactly what had happened. Dimia's room was filled with those now in the slumber. Rhys was on a cot, a blanket pulled up to his shoulders, his face still and peaceful. There were at least half a dozen others, though few seemed as badly injured as he was.

Elanor knelt on the floor next to him, holding his hand. She was to blame. She had forgotten her training. She hadn't been thinking when she left the palace, hadn't even bothered covering her tracks. She gave them a trail of bread crumbs and they followed her straight inside.

But the barrier. What about the barrier?

"Elanor." Brigid appeared in the doorway. Her face was ashen. "You need to come." Brigid took Elanor's hand. She couldn't tell who was trembling or if it was both of them. Elanor let herself be led.

Tasmin was already gone when they reached her.

Her body lay just outside the barrier, splayed across the gnarled roots of a tree. Elanor stumbled, her legs forgetting their purpose. She had thought there was no pain on earth unknown to her, but this, this was completely new. It was as if a thorn bush had taken root within her stomach, the sharp vines ripping her apart from the inside.

Thackery was standing guard, his head bowed. Dagger was curled up on Tasmin's chest, covering the wound that had no doubt killed her. The fox's fur was stained with blood, but she seemed unharmed. When Elanor lifted her carefully into her arms, Dagger whimpered but burrowed close. Elanor couldn't touch the body.

"We need to bring Tasmin inside," she said, amazed she could speak.

Thackery nodded, easily lifting the still form into his arms. Tasmin seemed so small when she was cradled this way, like a child. It took all Elanor's energy to follow them, to put one foot in front of the other. The vines kept growing inside her, dragging their sharp points along each rib. Elanor held

Dagger close, tighter than she should, but the fox made no protestations. The walk to the Mountain took seasons.

"What do we do now?" asked Brigid, once they had placed Tasmin next to the other dead. The huntsmen must have waited for her, ambushed her. They must have known where she was going to be and when.

Elanor didn't answer. Her chest was filled with thorns, but there was no time to mourn. No time to cry. She forced herself to think back, to remember what had happened. She had been sitting. No, she had been standing. Fighting. Fighting with Wren when the huntsman had appeared. He had grabbed her. Demanded to know where it was. It.

"Come with me," said Elanor. With Dagger balanced across her shoulders, and Brigid and Thackery at her heels, Elanor headed to Dimia's. The room was quiet and tense, healers leaning over those stretched out on cots. Aislynn saw them enter and came over to embrace Thackery. Her face was streaked with tears, but her eyes were clear and focused.

Elanor went straight to Rhys. Crouching next to him, she gently patted him down. It was gone. His dagger, the one he had taken from Benedict, was gone.

Elanor's weapons had been taken when she was in the palace, so she turned to Brigid and Thackery, who were looking at her with confusion.

"Did they take your weapons?" she asked. "When you were attacked, did they take your weapons?"

But she knew the answer just by looking at them. Both were still armed.

"They stole the dagger," said Elanor. "The one he took from Benedict. The huntsman asked me where it was, and then he attacked Rhys and took it. It's what they wanted. The dagger and chaos and confusion."

Everyone was silent. Elanor held the fox close, not minding the blood, just wanting to feel the warmth of another being. It didn't seem possible that all this destruction was for a single knife. There must be something else, something she was missing.

She looked at the others. Brigid was assisting Dimia, who was doing her best to heal the wounded while tears streamed down her face. Aislynn was on the floor with Cinnamon, trying to clean blood from the wolf's muzzle. There was a cut on her neck, but she didn't seem to notice. Thackery had disappeared.

"You're injured," Elanor told Aislynn, gesturing to her neck.

Aislynn placed her palm over the wound and closed her eyes. There was a soft pulse of magic, and when she lowered her hand, the cut was gone. She wiped away the blood.

Dagger moved from Elanor's shoulder to the mattress, settling against Rhys's cheek, her tail curling over the top of his head.

"Where's Thackery?" asked Elanor.

Thackery returned before Aislynn could reply. There was a cut on his forehead surrounded by a quickly darkening bruise. It hadn't been there the last time Elanor had seen him. Aislynn sprang to her feet and took his face in her hands.

"What happened?" she asked.

Elanor drew her weapon. "Are they back?"

"No." Thackery closed his eyes as Aislynn healed him. "Wren," he said.

"Wren?"

"She's gone," he said. "She went back to the palace."

*C*hapter .33

They made quick time to the palace, but it wasn't enough to catch up to Wren. None of them had said anything since they left the Mountain. Elanor had simply gathered up her weapons and departed, discovering along the way that the others had done the same. There was no plan. In fact, Elanor had not thought past their arrival at the tunnel. She just knew she needed to get Wren. And, if they were lucky, answers.

It had begun to snow, icy drifts coming down heavy and fast. One last storm before the spring. Their footprints were erased as soon as they made them, the sky above darkening swiftly. Elanor's clothes were soaked, ice finding a home beneath the collar of her jacket and sliding down her bare back. The briar wall was thickened by the white flurries, the sharp thorns hidden beneath the snow. When they reached the tunnel, they found it still exposed, but fresh blood was staining the ground. Wren was already inside.

One by one they crawled into the tunnel. Elanor was last. The darkness nearly overwhelmed her, but she made it through. Her weapons made the journey difficult, but she was unwilling to leave them behind. Who knew what they would encounter?

But the prison was deserted, the cells empty, doors ajar, and it didn't take them long to realize that there was no one on patrol. The ease with which they traveled concerned Elanor. She glanced at Thackery. It was clear he felt the same.

Elanor shivered, her clothes heavy and wet against her skin. A hand rested on her shoulder, and Brigid's magic swelled around her. In the space of a breath, she was dry and warm. Silently Elanor waited as Brigid did the same to the others, even Cinnamon, who was caked in dirt from the tunnel.

They climbed the stairs, their footsteps masked by the echo of water against stone, the walls wet and ceiling dripping. Unlike the music that filled the Mountain's cavern of mineral pools, this was a hollow sound, lonely and cold.

The door was wide open, and a gray light illuminated the

top of the stairs. Snow was coming down hard now. Brigid went first, cautiously leaning out into the cold air, bow drawn.

Everyone seemed to hold their breath. Elanor could hear her heartbeat in her ears, shivering despite her dry clothes. But when Brigid turned back to them, she had a look of utter disbelief on her face.

"It's empty," she said in a whisper. "There's no one there."

Elanor leaned forward. Surely there was someone in the courtyard, or a line of huntsmen up above on the walkway. Perhaps Brigid hadn't looked hard enough.

But when she peered out past the falling snow, she saw no one. Not a single soldier or guard. Not even a servant. No one.

"Something is wrong," she said to the others. Nothing about this felt safe.

"Maybe they were distracted by Wren," said Aislynn, reminding Elanor why they were there. Wren had most likely charged into the courtyard without a plan, fueled by rage and betrayal. But could she have captured the attention of every single huntsman guarding the palace?

Cinnamon pushed past Elanor's legs and trotted out into the courtyard, her paws making clear prints in the snow-covered ground.

"Cinnamon!" Aislynn whispered frantically, but the

wolf ignored her, taking steady, confident strides toward the entrance of the Queen's palace.

Once again Elanor held her breath, waiting for arrows to shower down around Cinnamon, but none came. The courtyard was truly deserted. Across from the prison, Elanor could see that the main gate was wide open. She followed the wolf, gesturing for the others to do the same. They made their way, back to back, weapons drawn. Any snow that touched them immediately melted away, Brigid's magic protecting them from the elements. The sky above was a fearsome silver, almost too bright to look at. Cinnamon waited patiently on the steps of the palace, her tail gently wagging.

With Thackery's help, Elanor managed to open the heavy iron doors, and they entered the castle.

The enormous room that served as the entryway was empty, as well. Without hesitating, Cinnamon headed up the stairs, her nails clicking on the stone floor. The palace seemed larger without anyone around, and their steps sounded in the empty hallway.

They went upstairs, still encountering no one. The silence was terrifying. It wasn't until they began heading toward the Queen's chamber that they caught sight of their first guard. He was standing at attention in front of a door. He was alone.

Everyone froze, but not fast enough.

The huntsman caught sight of them, his bow raised. But before he could fire the arrow or even call out, there was a clunk and he crumbled to the floor. A golden bookend in the shape of a harp rolled away from his prone form.

"Good aim," Brigid said to Thackery, who had thrown the knickknack.

"Shall we see what he was guarding?" he asked.

For a moment Elanor thought of continuing on and not bothering with the door. But it was the only place that was guarded in the otherwise abandoned palace. It must be important. Thackery quickly dispensed with the lock, and they all drew their weapons as he pushed open the door.

A young man was lying on a bed in the center of the room. Elanor saw red hair, and her heart jumped with unexpected relief. But then he turned over, and it was very clear that he was not the prince. His face was swollen and covered in dried blood, and on closer observation it was clear that despite the color of his hair, he didn't share any of Benedict's other attributes.

"Who are you?" Elanor demanded, shoving aside the worry that bubbled up inside of her.

"My name is Matthias." The decoy. He squinted at them and struggled to sit up. "Who are you?"

"Where is Cyril?" asked Elanor as Aislynn moved into the room.

"Where is the other Matthias?" she asked. Elanor glared at her.

"Benedict is with Cyril," said Matthias. "They took him about an hour ago." He was pale and sickly. "Please, tell me who you are."

"We're friends of his," said Aislynn, lowering her weapons and kneeling at his side. "He's badly hurt," she told the others.

"Take care of him," ordered Elanor. "We'll find Wren."

"Try the Queen's chamber." Matthias tried to get up, but Aislynn gently pushed him back.

Elanor nodded, and leaving Aislynn and Cinnamon with the true Matthias, she led Thackery and Brigid down the hall toward Josetta's chamber. The doors were wide open, and Elanor heard someone scream. Wren.

Elanor rushed into the room.

Wren was kneeling on the floor, facing the throne where Cyril sat, fingers at his forehead as if he had a headache. To his left was his son, as pallid and impassive as ever, and to his right Josetta and Benedict were seated, ankles and wrists chained.

For a brief moment, Benedict's gaze met hers. "Elanor, no!" he cried, his eyes pained.

Elanor quickly looked away, focusing on the scene in front of her.

The doors behind Elanor slammed closed. Magic crackled in the air, and she could hear Thackery and Brigid pounding on the doors and shouting for her.

"I always forget how inconvenient it is to kill someone with magic," said Cyril, almost conversationally, his other hand around Josetta's throat.

He looked up and smiled, as if seeing Elanor for the first time. He rose from the throne and came toward her, stopping alongside Wren, who had not moved.

"I don't ask for much," he said, placing a hand on Wren's shoulder. "Simple competence is all I want." He was holding Benedict's dagger, the one whose handle was adorned with jewels. The largest one seemed to be glowing faintly.

"Let me ask you if you can tell the difference between this weapon"—he raised his fist—"and *this* one." With a shove, he sent Wren toppling onto her back. Buried in her chest was the dagger Elanor had made, its simple hilt stained with blood.

Chapter .34

Elanor fell to her knees beside Wren, but it was too late. Above her she could hear Cyril talking, but the words barely registered as her shaking fingers closed Wren's eyes, which had been frozen in pain and terror.

"Such a shame. She was so angry, so eager to fight." Cyril returned to the dais. "I do appreciate loyalty, and she was quite useful for a time." Cyril turned to the Queen. "She hated you so much, my dear, she would have done anything to bring you down." Josetta was still seated, staring straight ahead, her expression completely blank. "You remember her, don't you?"

The Queen said nothing. Her neck was red. Raw.

"I suppose it doesn't matter," said Cyril, though frustration was beginning to show on his face. "She's served her purpose. And you—" He addressed Elanor, who had taken Wren's cold, stiff hand in her own. "You'll serve your purpose as well. Now, when all the bodies are discovered, it will be clear that this was an attack carried out by the rebels. Sadly my son and I will be the only survivors." He turned back to Josetta. "Shall we begin? I don't want to keep my future subjects waiting."

Her empty gaze had turned toward the ceiling.

"Come now," said Cyril, and Elanor could hear his teeth grinding together. "There's no point in your pride. We all know how this will end, and I, for one, would like to see you beg."

"We both know that's not what you want," said Josetta flatly.

Cyril's hand shot out, wrapping around the Queen's throat again.

"You think you know what I want?" He pulled her to her feet, bringing her face to his. Her shackles clanged. "Such a beautiful creature. But arrogant." Cyril smiled. "At first I only wanted the dagger." He held it out, the stone now glowing bright white. "But you built quite the kingdom, my Queen. Shame about your king, though." He looked over at Benedict. "Your father was in my way, you understand. But his death was more beneficial to the cause than I ever could have imagined."

"Stop it," said Benedict, struggling to stand, his chains trapping him in his chair.

The room buzzed with magic, and with a flick of his wrist, his hand still holding the dagger, Cyril seemed to force Benedict back down.

"I don't have to listen to you," Cyril sneered. "I don't have to listen to any of you."

Suddenly Benedict's eyes went wide and his hands strained against the shackles, fingers scrabbling toward his neck. It looked as if he was choking. Cyril's eyes were narrow, focused on the prince. Cyril's son watched from his seat, the hint of a smile playing on his lips.

"Stop it," shouted Elanor. "You're going to kill him!"

"That, my dear," Cyril said, his own face turning red from the exertion, "is the point."

"Stop!" Josetta's voice was hoarse, her throat still crushed beneath Cyril's fingers. There were strands of white threading through her hair that hadn't been there before. Her skin, too, looked as if it had aged, lines now visible around her mouth. "I beg of you," she said.

Immediately Cyril released his grip and Benedict slumped back in his chair, his breath ragged but steady—he appeared to be unconscious.

"What did you say?" Cyril asked Josetta. He was facing away from Elanor, his fingers resting loosely against Josetta's throat. His thumb traced the side of her neck.

"I begged you to stop," said Josetta, her voice unusually soft. "Please, let my son live."

Cyril shook his head. "You know I can't do that." But his attention was fully focused on the Queen.

"I beg you to make it painless, then," she said.

"What will you give me in exchange?" he asked greedily.

"What you've always wanted." Josetta leaned against him, practically purring. Elanor's skin crawled, and she saw that Cyril's son looked away, disgust evident on his face. "Me."

Cyril laughed. He grasped her cheeks and kissed her roughly. "I knew you would acquiesce." His voice was muffled as he buried his face in her neck. Elanor watched as Josetta's eyes narrowed into slits over Cyril's shoulder.

Her eyes caught Elanor's. They were full of urgency, her gaze darting downward. Elanor followed it to Wren's unmoving chest, where the simple dagger was still buried.

Cyril was murmuring into the Queen's neck. "The others never saw your potential," he said. "But I did."

Still focused on Elanor, the Queen wrapped her arms around Cyril, and Elanor watched as she placed her hand on his back, where his heart was. As Elanor pulled on the dagger, Josetta pressed herself closer to Cyril. On the dais, Cyril's son was unmoving, as if he too was under a spell, his eyes averted.

"From the moment I saw you, I knew," Cyril said. "We could have been magnificent together."

The blade was sticky in Elanor's hands, and she struggled to keep herself from retching at the feel of Wren's blood on her fingers.

Suddenly Cyril pulled away from Josetta. His back was still facing Elanor.

"You must think I'm a fool," he said. His son's gaze turned to the scene on the dais, flat eyes wide.

Josetta spat in Cyril's face. "You *are* a fool," she said. "You think I didn't know what you were after? And still, it took you forty years to get it." She sneered. "You and your friends—what idiots they were to send *you*. You always were the weakest. The most—"

"You witch!" screamed Cyril, grabbing Josetta's neck with one hand and pressing the dagger's blade against her throat with the other. Blood appeared on her pale skin, trickling down the bodice of her dress, staining the satin.

The stone on the dagger glowed and the walls began to shake. The windows rattled and the floor trembled. Elanor could feel magic all around her, so thick it threatened to choke her. Cyril's son remained immobile, his fingers clutching the chair. He was deadly pale.

"I thought so often of using your powers. The others told me to wait. Bide my time. But I thought about it each time I saw you," Cyril said, his knuckles white around the Queen's throat, around the dagger's hilt. "Wanting to possess your magic. To feel it. And now that I do, I must say, my dear, you don't disappoint."

Elanor watched with horror as Josetta began to age in Cyril's grasp. Her hair had gone almost completely gray, her skin crumpling like burned parchment. Her features were distorted, monstrous. But her eyes were sharp and remained focused on the blade now in Elanor's hand.

Elanor raised the weapon. Her hand was shaking, but when she released it, her aim was true.

Chapter 35

Cyril cried out as the knife struck him in the back. It went deep, blood staining his clothes. His hands fell away from Josetta's neck as he clawed for the curved blade between his shoulders, unable to reach it. Elanor watched as the Queen, now ancient and gray, ripped the jeweled dagger from his grip. She barely looked human anymore.

"You'll never use me again," she growled, and sliced the knife across his throat. As blood spilled from Cyril's neck onto her gown, Josetta thrust the blade into her own chest.

Cyril fell.

"Father!" Cyril's son, who had been frozen with shock, jolted forward, as if to catch the bodies. But there was only one.

Josetta had disintegrated when the dagger plunged through her heart, and her body disappeared in a puff of dust. Only her bloodstained gown and crown remained, clattering to the floor with the dagger. Blood spread from beneath Cyril's body, and he let out one last gurgle before his body lay still.

Elanor rushed to Benedict. He was breathing. While she tried to wake him, the doors slammed open as Brigid and Thackery burst in.

But before they could reach her the room filled with smoke. The air was thick with a strange bluish cloud, and Elanor couldn't breathe. She could hear the others but was unable to see them.

"Elanor?" Brigid cried out. "Where are you?"

The fog was opaque, too thick to see anyone. Elanor sensed someone moving toward her. But he didn't linger. Instead he shoved her aside and then quickly disappeared.

Cold air and magic pushed through the room, clearing the smoke. Cyril's son was gone, as was the jeweled dagger. Elanor scrambled to her feet and dashed out into the hallway. A figure was running away.

Suddenly Aislynn burst into the hall, bow and arrow at the ready, Cinnamon growling at her side.

"Westerly!" she cried, and fired the arrow. Elanor could

feel magic propelling it forward, carrying it farther than it should have gone, and faster.

The arrow struck Cyril's son in the arm. He stumbled but did not stop, and disappeared around the corner. Aislynn dashed after him, Elanor following.

But when Elanor turned the corner, expecting to see Aislynn and Cinnamon with Westerly trapped, she was surprised to find them alone, looking confused and angry.

"Where is he?" Elanor wheezed, trying to catch her breath.

"He just disappeared," said Aislynn. She threw down her bow and arrow with disgust. "Westerly! I should have known."

"Westerly?" Brigid came thundering up from behind them. "That was him?"

"Who is Westerly?" The name sounded familiar, but Elanor could not remember why.

Brigid and Aislynn exchanged a look.

"That was Linnea's husband," said Aislynn.

Chapter .36

There had been no sign of Westerly or of the dagger. The castle had been searched, dozens of secret passages and entrances discovered and then sealed, but nothing had given them any indication of where Linnea's husband had gone.

They buried Cyril in an unmarked grave. The Queen's funeral was left to Benedict, though Elanor knew some of the Orphans wished he would do the same. Aislynn told her that he buried her bloodstained gown, along with the foxtail coat and crown, beneath her lemon tree—the one that had been kept forever in bloom. Afterward the servant who had been tasked with making sure the tree continuously bore fruit was allowed to let it rest.

Benedict's friends, those who had traveled with him to the palace on that first journey, had been moved from the dungeons and were discovered locked in various rooms throughout the palace, though not all of them had been found. A young girl named Olivia, as well as several other women, had disappeared. No one seemed to know what had happened to them. According to the others, Olivia, who had cried every night, had simply gone silent one evening.

Elanor left the day after the burials, eager to leave the palace behind, eager to return home. But when she arrived at the Mountain, it didn't feel like home. It felt as it had when she first arrived all those years ago, unfamiliar and empty.

The barrier was gone. No one was strong enough to create a new one. And even though Josetta was dead and most of her huntsmen had fled, Elanor still felt exposed and vulnerable. She was lonely for Ioan, who would receive the news of Tasmin's death soon. And she was envious that he would have a family to comfort him when he did.

Sleep was long coming every night, and each morning she woke with a sick feeling in her stomach. In her dreams she was visited by all she had failed: Wren, Tasmin, and Rhys. It was Wren's face that haunted her most: those wide-open eyes, that cold, still body. Elanor could still feel the blood on her hands.

There was a pool in the Mountain, far deeper than any of

the bathing pools. It was cooler there, even in the summer, and it was where Orphans washed the dead before they were burned. It was an act performed by the person who needed to say good-bye the most. Bronwyn washed Wren's body; Elanor washed Tasmin's.

Tasmin was heavy in Elanor's arms when she lowered them both into the frigid water. Elanor ignored the cold. The wounds on Tasmin's body had been closed by Dimia, but they were still visible, still red against her skin. The slash across Tasmin's chest was the hardest to clean.

She washed Tasmin's hair and brushed it carefully when she was done. She made sure that her mother's body was clean, pure. Elanor had never been able to look closely at the ink on Tasmin's skin. Now she could see it—the seven swans across her arm, and seven names across her back. The names of her brothers, Elanor assumed. Seven brothers, now dead.

Tasmin would be wrapped in clean cloth and burned. The ashes would help feed the forest in the spring. The Orphans believed that this custom allowed those you loved to stay with you forever.

But Elanor knew it wasn't true. Tasmin was gone, and there was no getting her back.

Afterward Elanor went to the mineral pools and scrubbed her skin so hard that it hurt to put her clothes back on.

Nothing was the same now. Josetta was dead, and Elanor had helped destroy her. But that brought her no comfort. For so long she had thought of nothing but killing the Queen. She thought that she would feel free. But she didn't. She didn't feel anything.

Elanor sat in her room and stared at her forge. What would she make now? Everything she had ever made had brought sorrow and pain. She looked at her hands and all she saw was death. Everything she had ever done with them had brought unhappiness to others. A part of her wanted to crawl into the fire, to burn to ash as well. Perhaps she would be better as food for the forest. Perhaps she would finally be something good. Something useful.

She hated the Four Sisters. Hated that the Orphans thanked them for every battle won, because from where Elanor stood, there was no such thing as a battle won. The losses were too high, no matter who was victorious.

Elanor visited Rhys every day. Dimia kept him in the slumber while she waited for his shoulder to heal. There was a patch over his eye. The scars were deep, cutting from the middle of his eyebrow to the edge of his nose. He was still handsome.

When it was finally time to wake him, Elanor sat at his side and held his hand tight.

He woke much as Benedict had, gasping as if he had been

underwater, now finally reaching the surface. For a long time he didn't stir. Elanor sat and watched his chest moving up and down steadily. Finally he opened his eye.

"I thought it was a nightmare," he said, and began to cry.

Elanor held him until all his tears were gone.

Chapter .37

When the others returned to the Mountain, Benedict was with them.

"He wanted to come," Aislynn told Elanor. "He wanted to speak to you."

But Elanor refused to see him.

"He shouldn't be here," she told Rhys. He had his arm looped through hers and they were walking the perimeter, where the barrier had been. It was the first time he had been outside since being woken from the slumber. All around them were the signs of spring. Dagger dashed around their feet, nipping at the green shoots pushing through the melting snow.

"He might not have anywhere else to go," said Rhys, keeping a firm grip on her.

"Why doesn't he just stay in the Midlands palace?"

"Maybe it has unpleasant memories for him."

Elanor ignored him. "He shouldn't be here," she said again.

"Who are you punishing, Ellie?" Rhys stopped and faced her. She didn't let her gaze waver. "It's not your fault," he said.

But Elanor didn't believe him.

Aislynn had something to tell them. That night they gathered in the kitchen—Elanor, Thackery, Brigid, Rhys, and Aislynn. Dagger was curled up on Elanor's lap, Cinnamon on the floor, her ears drooping sadly.

"She's been this way since the burial," Thackery explained. "She stood next to the lemon tree and howled for an hour." Suddenly the wolf's ears perked up.

Benedict was standing in the doorway.

"What are you doing here?" Elanor demanded.

Cinnamon trotted over to him, her tail wagging.

"I'm sorry," he said, petting the wolf, who leaned heavily against his legs. "I thought—"

Aislynn stood. She had a copy of *The Path* in her hands.

"I invited him," she said. "I thought he might be able to help us."

Elanor was about to object, but Rhys spoke before she could.

"Have a seat, Ma—" He quickly corrected himself. "Benedict."

Benedict took a seat. Cinnamon curled up at his feet, her nose tucked beneath her tail. Some of her sadness seemed to be lifting.

"I think I discovered something," said Aislynn. "In your story of the Four Sisters, they are four warriors, each given new life as an animal after their sacrifice in battle." She opened the book to a page she had marked. "*The Path* tells of four sisters, as well. Only they are warnings of what a woman can become if she doesn't control her abilities. And in that story, the sisters each have an item that represents her folly." She pointed to the page. "A crown, a ring, a mirror, and a dagger." Aislynn turned to Elanor. "You said the dagger glowed, right?" she asked.

Elanor nodded. "One of the stones on the handle."

Aislynn looked at the others. "Just like the ring and the mirror."

"What ring?" asked Benedict. "What mirror?"

Aislynn pulled the mirror from her pocket and placed it on the table. There was a slight glow to the stone in the handle, which quickly faded. "I think these items are connected," she said. "And I think they all do the same thing. I think they can steal magic." She turned to Elanor. "You said that Cyril used magic."

"That's how he killed Wren," said Elanor, her throat burning. She remembered how Aislynn had told them of her adviser using magic, how he had wrapped his hands around her neck and it had felt like he was pulling magic from inside her. Elanor hadn't believed her. Now she wished she had taken the princess more seriously.

Aislynn turned to Benedict. "Cyril said that he had been looking for the dagger?"

Benedict nodded. "My mother gave it to me when she sent me away. After my father died." He swallowed hard. "After Cyril had him killed."

They had all been shocked to learn of Wren's association with Cyril. That he had been responsible for providing her with information about where huntsmen would be. He had been the one who told her the truth about the poison, for he had given it to Wren and then warned Josetta about it. He had been manipulating both sides for years.

"At some point, he found a way to take control of the throne, to convince some of my mother's huntsmen that he was the rightful ruler," Benedict continued.

Elanor remembered how the Queen had been absent from her usual public appearances. How the huntsmen had stopped trying to find the Orphans and instead started aggressively expanding the Midlands. But the reason behind Cyril's decision to do so, like so many things, remained unknown.

"Why, if he already had the power, did he keep your mother alive? Why didn't he just kill her instead of imprisoning her?" asked Thackery.

"I think he wanted the dagger," said Benedict. "And me. He wanted to kill both of us, to make it look like an assassination. He wanted to unite the huntsmen against you. Like when my father was killed. But he failed."

"Now you're next in line for the throne," said Aislynn.

"But it's not really my throne, is it?" said Benedict. "Just as it wasn't really my mother's."

Everyone was silent. What would happen to the Western Kingdom now that Josetta was gone? Would those royals who had been chased away return? Or would someone else come and try to take her place as Cyril had intended to do?

"And Westerly has the dagger," Thackery finally said.

"I assume he's taken it back to Hull," said Aislynn. "And I would bet a sack of beans that he won't stop looking for the mirror. The crown, too, if he doesn't already have it."

"So he can steal magic," Benedict said slowly.

Aislynn's face was grave. "I think so. But what scares me is, if all these items can do the same thing, if they can steal magic, why does he need all of them? What if there's something else, something worse that they can do when they're together?"

Chapter .38

Elanor escaped the meeting as soon as she could, her head swimming. Hadn't they just ended a war? It seemed that all it had given them was a new enemy and a new mission. A stolen dagger. A missing crown. Maybe she wasn't meant for peace. Maybe this was what the Four Sisters expected from her. Wanted from her.

The air was fresh and bright in her lungs when she came out of the Mountain and headed into the forest. All Elanor wanted was to feel the sun against her face, breathe in the scent of pine and spring. But she was not alone. Knife drawn, Elanor whirled around to find Benedict standing there. She didn't lower her weapon.

"Elanor—" he said, hands raised in surrender.

"I don't want to speak to you," she said.

"I just wanted to apologize."

"For what?" Elanor asked. "For your lies? For your betrayal? Was any of it the truth?"

"Yes." Benedict lowered his eyes. "I lied about my name. And about being the prince. But everything else was the truth."

She didn't believe him. "You said the Queen gave you the brand on your shoulder."

"The truth."

"You told me that you barely knew your mother."

"I wasn't raised in the palace. My mother—" He stopped. "She told me that I should be grateful that she cared enough to protect me." The words were so familiar, so similar to what Josetta had said to Elanor in the dungeon, that she shivered. But she was not ready to be forgiving.

"Did you know what she was doing to us?"

"No," said Benedict. "I knew I was meant to inherit the throne from her, but I knew nothing of how she ruled. Of how she intended me to rule."

"Were you ever going to tell me? Or did you go with Wren so that you didn't have to?"

Shame flooded Benedict's face. "I wanted to find my

mother. To stop her. To make things different."

"And now? What will you do now?"

"I don't know," said Benedict. "I don't know where my place is anymore. I don't know where I belong." He looked at Elanor. "I'm sorry. I'm so sorry." Benedict reached for her, but Elanor moved away.

It still hurt. Maybe it would always hurt. "You lied to me."

"I know."

He turned to go, but before she could stop herself, Elanor grabbed his arm. "Stay with me. Just for a little longer," she heard herself say. She didn't want to be alone.

So they stood there, in the warm sun. And when Benedict linked his fingers with hers, she didn't hold them tight, but she didn't let go, either.

That night she lay in bed, staring through the darkness. She saw nothing. It was so dark that she wasn't even sure she was awake. She didn't know if she wanted to be awake. Sleep was full of nightmares. Benedict, standing in front of his mother. The Queen growing old and turning to dust. Tasmin curled on the ground, broken and small. And Elanor saw her own hands. Her own bloodstained hands.

Elanor felt Dagger brushing against her leg as the fox made her way up the bed. Elanor waited for her to do what she usually did and settle across her neck, but Dagger climbed onto her chest instead. Even though it was dark, Elanor could feel the fox staring down at her from her new perch.

"What?" Elanor finally asked, even though she knew the animal could not answer her. "What do you want from me?"

Dagger's paws prodded her. What was she doing? Then she began turning in circles and Elanor jerked back as the fox's tail brushed against her face.

Finally Dagger settled, curling up into a ball on Elanor's chest.

At first Elanor didn't understand. Dagger had always slept in the same place, draped across her neck. Then Elanor remembered why. She reached up and felt for the scar on her throat. It was the same it had always been. A reminder of how she could have died but didn't. Dagger had slept against that scar for as long as it had existed.

"She's trying to heal you." Tasmin's words came through the darkness.

Dagger knew where the pain was and she was going to make it better. The little fox was doing what she knew how to do. She was trying to help.

But this wasn't an injury that would heal. This wasn't something that would close up and fade. It was a permanent break, a forever wound.

"You can't make it better," Elanor whispered, and Dagger lifted her head at the sound. "You can't fix this."

The fox nudged at Elanor's chin. She seemed to be saying, I'm not here to fix it; I'm here to make it bearable.

The numbness lifted off Elanor, like a shroud being removed. Grief flooded her and the tears came, hot and unending. It was time. It was time to forgive herself.

And then came a strange sensation between her ribs. Magic. It had never felt this way before. Faint, but steady. It was like being woken from the slumber. The darkness and nightmares—the loss of Tasmin—lingered, but there was light ahead. A chance to heal.

Elanor was never going to be a girl without scars. She was never going to be fixed. But she would fight. And she would survive.

Josetta's Lemon Tart

A wickedly tart dessert that will burn your tongue.

INGREDIENTS

For the candied lemon slices:

1 lemon

¾ cup sugar

¾ cup water

For the crust:

½ cup sugar

¾ cup butter, softened

1 large egg yolk

2 cups unsifted cake flour

For the filling:

4 large egg yolks

¾ cup sugar

4 tablespoons lemon juice

½ cup unsalted butter, cut into small pieces

DIRECTIONS

Make the candied lemon slices:

1. Mix sugar and water in a saucepan over medium heat until sugar dissolves and water is boiling.

2. Reduce heat to low and add the lemon slices.

3. Simmer until lemon slices are translucent, about 30 minutes.

4. Remove pan from heat and allow syrup and lemons to cool.

5. Once cool, remove the lemon slices from the pan and allow them to dry on a wire rack.

Make the crust:

1. Cream together the sugar and butter, using first a wooden spoon and then a fork to beat them together. (This can also be done in a food processor or with an electric mixer.)

2. Once the ingredients are yellow, fluffy, and well incorporated, add the egg yolk and flour.

3. Press the dough into a 9 ½-inch greased tart pan with your fingers.

4. Bake at 325 degrees for 25–30 minutes or until lightly browned.

5. Allow to cool.

Make the filling:

1. In a saucepan, use a rubber spatula to mix together the yolks, sugar, lemon juice, and butter over a medium-low heat for about 12 minutes. Butter should be melted and mixture thick.

2. Remove from heat and allow to cool.

3. Pour filling into the cooled pie crust.

4. Arrange candied lemon slices on top.

Enjoy!

(Josetta's Lemon Tart was adapted from tart and crust recipes in *Sunset* magazine and the recipe for lemon slices at www.youaremyfave.com/2013/05/31/a-lemon-tart-with-candied-lemons-is-my-fave)

Acknowledgments

To everyone who read and supported *Stray*. I am so grateful for your love and encouragement. *Burn* is for you.

To my agent, Samantha Shea. I adore you and am so happy you're on this journey with me.

To my editor, Virginia Duncan, and everyone at Greenwillow Books and HarperCollins. To Gina Rizzo, Katie Fee, and Preeti Chhibber. Thank you for all that you do.

To Margot Wood, the best cheerleader an author could hope for.

To everyone in the YA world, especially Brandy Colbert, Sarah Enni, Maurene Goo, Robin Benway, Tess Sharpe, MaryElizabeth Summers, and Brandon Hoang. I am so lucky to be part of a community as warm and wonderful as this one. There is nothing better than knowing I share (or will soon share) a place on the shelf with each of you.

To my family. My parents, my siblings, and all the friends and family who gave me confidence when I was running low. You made this possible.

To my favorite guy, John Petaja. Love you, dude.

And to Basil Pesto Poledouris Sussman-Petaja. You are still a dog and you are still awesome.

Don't miss *Stray*
by Elissa Sussman

A gorgeous companion novel to *Burn*!

Greenwillow Books
An Imprint of HarperCollinsPublishers